D0362232

SEVERO SARDUY

Firefly

Translated from the Spanish by Mark Fried

archipelago books

Copyright © 1990 by Severo Sarduy
English language translation © 2013 by Mark Fried

First Archipelago Books Edition, 2013

All rights reserved. No part of this book may be reproduced or transmitted in
any form without the prior written permission of the publisher.

First published as *Cocuyo* by Colección Andanzas in 1990.

Archipelago Books
232 3rd Street #A111
Brooklyn, NY 11215
www.archipelagobooks.org

Library of Congress Cataloging-in-Publication Data
Sarduy, Severo.
[Cocuyo. English]
Firefly / by Severo Sarduy ; translated from the Spanish by Mark Fried. –
1st Archipelago Books ed.
p. cm.
ISBN 978-1-935744-64-1
1. Transvestites – Fiction. 2. Gender identity – Fiction. 3. Cuba – Fiction.
I. Fried, Mark. II. Title.
PQ7390.S28C6413 2013
863'.64 – dc23   2012031993

Distributed by Consortium Book Sales and Distribution
www.cbsd.com

Cover art: Rufino Tamayo

The publication of *Firefly* was made possible with support from the
Spanish Ministry of Culture; Lannan Foundation; the National Endowment
for the Arts; the New York State Council on the Arts, a state agency;
and the New York City Department of Cultural Affairs.

CONTENTS

So no one will know I'm afraid 9

To become somebody else 25

Lack of air 49

A stable thought between two bouts of lunacy 63

Haven't you ever seen a bat smoke? 75

Firefly out cold 87

Poem from Plaza del Vapor 97

The urge to laugh 115

Disillusion 123

Wall tiles, with bony dance band 135

It's going to snow 141

The Pavilion of the Pure Orchid 151

Firefly

So no one will know i'm afraid

Wait, who is that guy with the big head? Firefly? My god, I thought he'd be more developed, not so skinny. I had imagined him sort of like a tiny Greek athlete with clear glass eyes and gold nipples.

I find him like this, all of a shocking sudden, squatting on his clay chamber pot, the pale gray one with two handles, atop a dark green cistern in the shade of a royal poinciana collapsing from the weight of the cockatoos. The first thing I see is his oversized head. And his eyes are so Chinese, he might as well not have any. A bald Chinaman. When he spreads his little arms, his chest is really scrawny: a spidery map of bones.

Instead of getting off the pot, he holds tight to both handles and lets himself slide down the cistern, and the basin shatters into more bits of ceramic than you'd find in a Julian Schnabel self-portrait. The cheeks of Firefly's bottom are two purple splotches

when he dashes across the various blues of the floor tiles, scream-
ing at the top of his lungs.

The three aunts are in such a tizzy from his descent you would
think they'd seen a polka-dotted bear cub riding a chariot down
a steep brambly slope.

The aunts: all in shining silk. There must be some baptism
to attend, or a small parish celebration. They gleam so in the
noonday sun that you have to squint to look at them. That isn't
all: crocodile-leather high heels with red platforms and over their
shoulders see-through handbags like round canteens for a thirsty
outing.

The make-up is simple: a bit of powdered eggshell does it, plus
a purple touch of Mercurochrome on the lips. Yes, it must be a
catechism klatch, or maybe the arrival from the mother country
of some buff parish priest whose photograph they've seen, the
longed-for replacement of the insipid confessor of bilious believers his predecessor turned into after half a century of evangelizing
against the tide.

And when I say against the tide I'm understating it: futile were
the supplications that efficaciously unleashed sonorous down-
pours, futile the holy water dispensed right and left that instantly
healed cankers and ulcers and even the cattle's aphthous fever,
and futile too the Hail Mary mediations that worked wonders

for soured engagements or serial infidelities. The catechumens always returned to their venerable orishas, hidden on the top shelf of their armoires – the inheritance, along with the cinnamon skin and thick lips, of some Maroon ancestor if not of a great-grandfather who, being from Africa itself, was respected in the neighborhood as a man *black by birth*.

Let's get back to the three dazzling women. The hairdo merits special attention: piled high of course, but in successive silvery waves that whipped the crown into a veritable ocean of white-caps. Haughty, necks erect, and so much hair spray not a wisp could budge. The three heads, turned in unison to watch Fire-fly's chamber-pot slide, were like burnished sculptures made of mother-of-pearl and aluminum: goddesses, no doubt; fairies, not likely; how about philanthropic *ladies* who assist the underprivi-leged, or famous but honest actresses. The giveaway was the lack of eye makeup or even a beauty spot above the lip. And if they smoked, it was on the sly.

But on to Firefly, who, though reflected in others and at times deformed by them, is the true subject of this pack of lies. Why did he launch himself down the cistern on that "fecal sled"? Let's see . . .

For me, he felt his aunts' gaze riddling him from the trenches of their eyes, the blinding sheen of their silks like silvery headlamps, their index fingers bejeweled with dazzling amethysts pointing, "Look at him! Look at him! Shitting in the cistern!" He was a tiny defecating Saint Sebastian, pierced by an arrow in the midst of his misdeed, the ass-shitting butt of their joke, a helpless stench.

It was his first fright. The stare: a pricking of pins dipped in curare that kept on sticking him, crucifying him, petrifying him alive up there on his double throne.

He pressed his arms against his sides as if he were having his picture taken. He felt paralyzed. He wanted to sink into the cistern for good, to drown amid frogs and water worms, to descend to the iridescent green sediment in the depths, and then, crossing through the clay bottom, to bury himself in the crust of mineral earth, ferruginous and cold, and there remain, curled up, a sandy fetus or a rusty mummy: *prenatal and posthumous at the same time.*

Nailed to the cistern was a wooden lid he could not raise. So then he wanted to fly, to nest in the reddish branches amid the muteness of bustling birds and the stridency of cockatoos, protected by the broad yellow-veined leaves; a coiled boa would defend the trunk. But the defecation dragged him down, robbing something of his very essence. It tied him to the cistern; he was sewn to the earth.

It was that double dead end that made him opt for the diagonal chamber-pot descent.

The three glittering women, now that they saw him running across the floor from one blue tile to another like a crazed bishop, heading toward his mother, who by now was waiting with open arms at the end of the hallway (she was yelling something but no one could make out what), turned to one another and reached their right hands down and forward in a wave, as if to indicate a nosedive or the pecking of a sandpiper.* Then they raised their hands to the heavens and shook them along with their heads, as if saying, "No!"

Firefly's mother was in a room set aside for weaving, at a spinning wheel beside a loom with skeins of colored yarn on spindles; strands of every color hung there, ready to be woven into a rug.

As he calmed down, the melon-head made up for his first phobia by producing his first eloquence: "Millimeter, decimeter, and centimeter!" he exclaimed.

Hearing him, the mother of that orthophonic issue could but cross herself. "Who," she scolded him, shaking him by the

* "The sandpiper dies blind," says Gustavo Guerrero. A fisherman from Laguna de la Restinga, on Margarita Island in Venezuela, once told him their eyelids get scorched from all that pecking in salt water.

shoulders and fixing him with a ferocious glare, "taught you those barbarities?"

She wiped his bottom with a sponge soaked in vinegar.

She sat him in a little wicker chair.

(A milky and bluish light, which showed up the dust in the air from the velvet upholstery, entered through the thick panes of the mullioned window to the left of the chair.)

She made him drink a mug of hot chocolate.

Silently, Firefly watched the open carts go by in the street. The horses' yellow excrement soiled the cobblestones; the clop of their hooves filtered through the window and into the room. He spied, perhaps in the distance like a toy, the train to the provinces climbing the black wooded hills and staining the blue morning air with compact puffs of coal dust and smoke.

The mother continued spinning. The wheel seemed to turn by itself.

What drove it, in reality, was a tabby cat playing with an invisible mouse. Or maybe with the spirit of one of the rodents people exterminated daily. The city was so infested with them that by night it was all theirs. They materialized at dusk in slow processions of shining eyes, as if drawn by the odor of the sea. They would not leave until dawn, dragging to the depths of the sewers the repugnant bits of all they had gained in the laborious night of incessant, abject gnawing.

Each family kept a rat potion of its own invention (the beasts were invulnerable to store-bought ones, immune to all known poisons), which they spread among the armoires and under the beds before retiring and kept in the pantry alongside bunches of onions hanging from the rafters, whole hams for Christmas Eve, copper frying pans, and one or more seven-armed Toledo lamps, vestiges of a nearby antique dealer gone bankrupt or a long-past fire in some synagogue.

It did not end there. A few days later, as tends to happen among these drifting islands – hollow rafts, borne by their own weight – the sky grew ugly. Yes, Tiepoloesque nimbuses, silvery gray with golden trim, began to roll in, whipped up on rising, spinning whirlwinds from the east. Gusts from the north, sly and freezing, whistled around corners and snatched up wedding bonnets with their hummingbird brims and bunches of varnished cherries. From the west came a downdraft, sweet and bluish like the smoke from a Partagás Culebra, carrying the scent of dense, freshly cut tobacco leaves, wrinkled and leathery and thickly veined. From the south, finally, a strange and to all appearances enemy rumbling, whose provenance and meaning no one could decode, reached the city. It was a distant choral murmur filled with muffled stridencies and mute clamors, as if from the grayish vault of the sky condemned angels were falling with heartrending shrieks. Or even closer: as if children were being slaughtered under a ceiba tree.

People nailed shut their doors and windows and shrouded their mirrors with black cloths when the screams of the souls reached their ears, because only an incorporeal and tortured army could give rise to such an interminable wail.

"It's the innocent children murdered by the Inquisition," they said, "back to demand justice. Their bodies are mangled but those are the voices they had in life, for the voice is all that remains intact after death."

"What innocents, what horseshit!" Making his first appearance in this story, throwing open the door of the living room, only to slam it shut with a bang that nearly shatters the windowpanes, is the father of the melon-headed chatterbox. "This is hurricane season!"

The storm that soon materialized gave rise to the fragile fast-talker's second phobia. And his most shrewd "performance."

It all began with a big party; island parties are sad and tumultuous. The women wore pants (they had started the day haggard

and short-tempered, drinking highballs and reading their horo-
scopes), plush kerchiefs on their heads and on their feet big
wooden clogs like stilts to keep them high and dry.

Neighborhood bands were blowing. What reigned was the sort
of disorder, the sort of dirty-undershirt impudence that happens
on days of national mourning or general strike. Without the least
hint of shame, the drunks sitting on street corners opened bottles
of beer in full view (which they later tossed into the storm sewer)
and guzzled them with a queasy grimace and in one long swill
(taunting hand in the air, all lit up) to keep them from getting
warm.

The old blacks had carried their flimsy little domino tables into
the street to escape the stale dank heat that sticks to your skin
between gusts. Straddling unsteady chairs, they banged their tiles
down with such fury that it seemed they would sink the whole
board. They cursed, *swearing they would have a white woman*;
they spit on the ground; they drank alarmingly long gulps of
harsh rum while awaiting a fresh breeze.

Every hour, they tuned into the weather report from the
observatory. On the radio, a meteorologist priest offered contra-
dictory indications of the tempest's trajectory. Firefly, needless
to say, interpreted for his sister (the only one accomplished at
deciphering the boy) the cleric's convoluted predictions, which,

[17]

while both cautious and learned, avoided with precise paraphrases any possible mishap.

"The hurricane's path," the priest asserted in a metallic voice made for the big-time microphone as well as the pulpit's echo, "traces a spiral opening up from its origin. Before it peters out it will head north, like migrating birds after the thaw. The danger lies in the voracious calm of the vortex, that innermost silence that announces the second lashing. Of course," he concluded modestly, "no hurricane travels on rails, so regarding the time of arrival . . ."

The sister, best known as "the Galician mouse" because that is how she dressed up for burials or when they were alone at home or to alleviate the no less funereal boredom of school assemblies and carnival celebrations, followed every detail of Firefly's hand signals with her questioning eyes, while the adults, gigantic puppets in clean clothes with brusque gestures and grating voices, drank endless cups of linden-flower or basil or peppermint tea to appease the anticipated nervous collapse.

At noon, grave and furrow-browed, the family and those close to them gathered in the weaving room, near the window whose panes had disappeared under a striped black-and-white convolution, crucified with tape and court plaster against the winds. On the great mahogany cabinet they tuned in the station of the observatory. Listening to the cleric's gongoristic dispatches, they made conflicting calculations to deduce the possible hour of the disaster.

The sister tiptoed close and touched Firefly affectionately on the shoulder, seeking an explanation with the deference of a dog putting his paw on his master's thigh and nudging with his head in pursuit of a lump of sugar.

"Bats," the melon-head then whispered into her ear, lingering on the sound with the gravity of one who has found the solution to an enigma. "Bats flew by."

They looked at each other then with astonishment.

Both paled.

They heard on the roof, light as acrobatic cats, new blasts of air.

In one holy amen the hurricane blew in like an Aeolus possessed. The sea turned wild and the crests of the waves soared as if spewing great wads of spit against the colonial façades on the far side of the street. Birds screeched, flying low to the ground. The palm trees began to bend until their crowns touched the roofing tiles.

Holding the circular shutter of the oxeye that usually ventilated the room open just a crack (they never opened the window, nor do I think they could have: the heavy sliding bolts were merely a decorative whim of affected architects), each by turn contemplated and conveyed to the rest, openmouthed and dying for news, the windswept panorama that surrounded them.

One by one they climbed a folding stepladder and used all their strength to hold the shutter tight and keep a devastating gust from slipping in and sweeping away the paintings, the faded map with Gothic letters and a single continent, and the central spiderlike copper chandelier strewn with the stubs – soft stalactites – of old tapers.

People were still in the street. The raconteur on the perch with a stiff-as-a-board disparaging style critical of everything was one of the aunts; the other two, from below, punctuated her lapidary phrases with cunning adjectives and empty sneers, which they wielded like amulets against fear.

An entire family was fleeing under a glossy white waterproof tablecloth. Arms open wide, the father held two corners of the protective rectangle aloft. The tablecloth shivered furiously, as if shaken by choleric titans; the crying progeny huddled underneath. They banged on every door they found, pleading for shelter.

An aunt, from below, sarcastically: "As if they hadn't had plenty of warning about the calamity! As if the silverware hadn't started turning green three days ago and the dogs hadn't lost their appetite and sense of direction! Well, since they paid no heed, let the wind carry them off!"

The other, farther up, after a moment of silence: "Nothing, nothing's happening and that's the worst of it. An insufferable calm . . ."

Then it was Firefly's turn to be the reporter. And it was not that he was already privy to the objective – in reality, sarcastic and vile – world of adults; no, more that he had his own eloquence, his own precision, for moments like this. Such a mature child for his age! The proof: an inured Rosicrucian who once ran into him in the street touched his forehead and exclaimed, "Here shines a light, the light of intelligence!"

So the melon-head climbed laboriously up the stepladder. His sister seemed to hold him up with her gaze. He reached the lookout. Under the rain, the city was like a weaving with diagonal stripes and all the colors pulverized, glued onto a white cardboard backing.

Little did his supposed fluency serve him. It turns out that sometimes, faced with what has to be said, words seem to soften and hang, flaccid and dripping saliva like the tongues of the hanged. What Firefly saw through the oxeye, as they say, had no name. He opened and closed his mouth like a harpooned porgy, trying to convey the scene to the inquiring chorus. But nothing came out. I'll try to say it myself, in the most neutral way I can to avoid any possible *humiliation of that speechless boy*.

The wind blew with such force it sliced off the eaves. Roofing tiles flew by, red stains, like pomegranate seeds in the gray of the rain; they smashed against the plinths and the ceramic façades. Hail beat against the big swathed window with a raucous metallic rat-a-tat, minuscule tin drums.

That much Firefly was able to recount – in his own way of course, and in a stuttering stammering fashion – to the gathering that longed fervently for cleverness and received his words with a thousand mocking sniggers. What he could not recount is what happened next: how one of the roofing sheets first opened up like the blade of a jackknife, and then slid down and took off, a leaf of zinc that flipped halfway in the air and shone like a silver dagger before diving straight down like a bolt of lightning . . . and slicing off the head of a black man running with a suitcase in his hand.

In the illusions of the circus (Firefly had gone to a matinee performance of the Santos y Artigas), the head cut off at a drum roll settled imperturbably back on the neck of the plump albino woman who undertook this remarkable exploit daily; that of the black man under the hailstorm fell smiling onto the suitcase that the decapitated body continued to hold.

Firefly tried to speak, but could not. His right hand rose and fell, again and again, like someone chopping down a tree. He had become mechanized, a windup toy, voiceless.

[22]

Then he felt something not only invade him icily through his feet, tying all his nerves in knots, but mix in with his very body, spilling out all over, like a shroud of sweat and cold.

He looked away from the blood-spattered circus, but it was too late: his legs trembled, his teeth chattered like castanets, he stared off into space like someone cross-eyed or hallucinating, hearing voices. The stepladder itself began to wobble, as if a benign earthquake were shaking the foundations of the house, rather than a hurricane its rooftop.

Seeing him like that, so stricken and mute, his face mottled with streaks spreading like angry little snakes, the family, as always when faced with a defenseless rara avis, redoubled its cruelty.

The aunts launched into a derogatory dance – because a little boy must not go soft – and the cackling cripples, like deboned Graces, parodied his vacillations and silence by mamboing in unison while emitting chortles, cachinnations, and stuttering shrieks.

The father kept repeating, "For the love of God, for the love of God!" yanking on the tip of a Havana with his teeth and draining compulsive cups of cognac.

The mother worked the empty spinning wheel and began to sway senselessly in a rocker piled with cushions, the haunt of parturient she-cats.

The sister took him by the arm to help him climb down the last steps. She whispered in his ear, affectionately, "How about some linden-flower tea? Or the *Golden Book of Animals* to take your mind off it?"

The butt of the adults' ridicule gave no answer. He fled sobbing to the kitchen, hunched over, hiding his face.

Once in the kitchen, using the cloth for drying the porcelain, he wiped away two big tears.

The buffeting winds were barely audible in there, but the brass pots hanging from the wooden rafters tinkled.

He counted the members of the family.

He prepared cups of linden-flower tea. For all, except himself.

He sprinkled them generously with rat poison.

With the utmost care, he laid them on a tray.

"So no one will know I'm afraid."

To become somebody else

Around a fountain, as if drawn by its cool waters, the feverish patients lie under archways on wobbly cots with no more accoutrements than a few mosquito nets of coarse tulle rolled up on spindles during the day and unfurled at night to reach the brick floor.

Beside the beds stand large copper pitchers for their ablutions, as well as bowls, enema hoses, white ceramic jars with green unguents, a sieve of vein-hungry leeches swimming over one another, and an archipelago of cotton swabs stained with pus, saliva, and blood. Farther off, an amphora of wine. A crystal vase with an iris.

Muscular nuns with ruddy cheeks and severe mannerisms make their rounds under the archways in a perpetual scurry and always in the same direction, collecting refuse and tendering salves and consolation, or little wool sacks with camphor stones, which they slide brusquely under the pillows.

Carefully, they close the eyes of the moribund and tie their jaws up with white cloths so that rigor mortis will not catch them by surprise; they give the thirsty salt to suck; they oblige those suffering boils or anemia to gulp a gelatinous and searing fish soup, which they shove at them with an enormous wooden spoon.

So heavily starched are the edges of their polyhedral cornets that the patients fear getting sliced open when the nuns go rushing by, busy as leaf-cutter ants throughout the night.

In the courtyard, next to the central fountain and spattered by its spray, stood a whipping post. Sick children frolicked around it and leaned contentedly against it, like someone playing on a swing unaware it was once a gallows.

The seven recent arrivals occupied an entire side of the square formed by the archways framing the courtyard. Firefly was in front. Wearing loose trousers, he lay on an unmade cot with a very heavy pillow across his feet.

The rest of the family floated in limbo, laughed in dreams, snored in chorus, praised or battled invisible interlocutors, caught a glimpse perhaps of the paradise to which all believers aspire and which often takes the form of a garden in full bloom.

The chief and only physician of the provincial hospital called on two retired luminaries of the island's medical community and begged them to join forces to decipher the enigma of this family, delivered from the recent disaster only to be plunged into a bottomless and immutable "post-cyclonic hypersomnia."

Let's watch the two healers from behind, strolling along a promenade bordered by royal palms up to the doorway, where the doctor greets them with only a simple embrace then points the way with a gesture of therapeutic impotence.

But, before we go on, who are these providential practitioners? To us, they appear as if in yellowed photographs or old faded postcards, surrounded by their appurtenances, their favorite gadgets, like peasants at a fair with the wooden cigarettes, desiccated cockatoos, sailors' caps, or tin rings, all provided by the photographer and yet true to the subject's identity.

First Gator, the herbalist, who collects the most paraphernalia.

Gator is wearing what looks like a dark blue suit with white pinstripes, round wire-rim glasses, and a silk tie decorated with tiny four-leaf clovers. His shoes are made of his own skin.

More worthy of mention is the place where he makes his appearance: in an orthopedic chair. Not that he is crippled, not at all; though he is lean and olive-skinned, long and bony, all obtuse angles and kinks, there is nothing unhealthy about him. His sallow disjointed face and that habit of sliding his index finger from his upper lip to his cheekbone are just his normal peculiarities. This phyto-practitioner, or herbalist to be more precise, has conserved (no one really knows why) all the therapeutic artifacts of bygone days when, rather than obey nature in its tortuous designs, he set his mind to using the most polished and austere of mechanical devices to oblige it to follow his own.

His house – floral lamps, arabesque banisters, opaline stained glass in that mother-of-pearlish vegetal style, all curves, which exaggeratedly typified art nouveau in the colonies – is brimming with dried plants in tiny envelopes of all colors, and crammed with the jumbled remains of all that clinical hardware, whose lines, authoritarian in their rectitude, interrupt the slow impinging curl of the crystal volutes.

Carpeting the bathroom are the most ludicrous of tiles made of bright ceramic, each containing dried eucalyptus leaves, bitter melon, nettles, or star apples in their two colors. The sink overflows with a greenish infusion made of cashew seeds, which keeps away wrinkles and gray hair. Two swan beaks are draining in the bidet.

This veggie-doc eats at a table with a well for a charcoal fire, covered by a dragonfly-and-lily patterned cloth, in the center of which sits an opaque, oval-shaped Galle vase filled with iridescent lilies. In a crosshatched physiotherapy mirror he spies on his own moves, as if they were those of a twisted competitor in a feverish game of crepuscular solitaire. He lays out the cards on a dissecting table.

Gator, as the assiduous reader would have noted by now, lives alone, but it is as if he were married to himself. He is a dreamer given to meditative mulling, for whom daily plant collecting, undertaken with the strabismic gaze of someone tracking the meandering flight of a butterfly with damp wings, is a search for primogenital purity or the unpredictable diversity of the planet.

Early in the morning, in an ablutionary reversal of his rural peregrinations, he masturbates, flipping through a French magazine filled with naked bodies and brief captions.

Then the dissident medic examines himself in the crosshatched mirror and organizes his thoughts about the day's practice, about using a burning mustard plaster to pull the malady out by the root. And with daily devotion, almost fear, he revisits the album of "Sicilian photos" by Baron Wilhelm von Gloeden, his secret mentor, his role model.

Today's exertions have exhausted him. He opts for a brew of

guasima bark, which he sips through a cinnamon straw. Once again he contemplates his unclothed image in the mirror as he wished never to have seen it. He touches the back of his hand to his incipient, rather white beard. With his index finger, he caresses his upper lip and then out along his cheekbone, tracing as if there were a straight line marked on his skin. He decides, at least for today, not to shave. At this juncture he no longer cares if they laugh at him, point at him in the street, and shout, "Gator's got a beard!"

Among the baron's yellowing photographs he selects one for unhurried contemplation that is particularly lascivious: two Sicilian lads, Hellenized with laurels and sandals, are about to touch breasts; between them, hieratic and naked, an adolescent girl in profile gazes at the heavens.

Isidro is the one who teaches anatomy. He lives surrounded by diligent attendants. For strictly pedagogic reasons, and with the compulsion of a bulimic foreseeing scarcity, he collects cadavers, which he bargains for at the morgue when no one is looking.

He is obese. When he returns from his lugubrious bazaar he stinks of formaldehyde and body odor. He shuffles about in battered flip-flops that the corner cobbler and his big mulatto make for him, not without plenty of teasing and a bit of remorse, deforming exquisite Italian shoes with hammer blows so that his swollen feet will fit and even find some consolation under that pile of blubber.

So pervasive was the anti-dictatorial chaos in Upsalón U, so predictable the daily rallies, muggings, knifings, and gunfights, and so precarious and early-morning the formal medical schooling, that sawbones-in-training would come by the dozen to the mouse-infested grotto Isidro had built in his own home so that he could share, with those willing to pay, his Frenchified skills in the pestilent art of dissection.

At sundown in the homespun lecture theater, wearing starched white lab coats and exhibiting the manners of unctuous bishops ("Medicine is a priesthood"), they received the anatomical rudiments that years later would earn them a license to heal.

Armed with a pointer, a series of colored slides, and a memorized translation of Testut's *Anatomie*, duly peppered with apothegms from Mesmerian electricism, the tub of lard projected diagrams of the alternating current that secretly joins the pylorus to the cardiac orifice, the voltaic arc that leads from auricles to ventricles, or the intermittent magnetism that simultaneously communicates and divides the two hemispheres of the brain. He had sketched these intensities on the transparencies as perfect discontinuous curves, like those made by iron filings between two magnets or under the rotation of a cone-shaped pendulum.

In the kitchen beside the amphitheater – between the two rooms, a beaded curtain clicked and quivered from the obsessive pacing of a mangy dog – an oniony and in her own way anatomical woman from Galicia, hair in a double bun and frying pan in hand, slaughtered chickens, fried up shrimp in red sauce, and baked biscuits with butter for the frugal meal of the man in flip-flops.

When he tired of the Galician's coarse dishes, or on Sundays, which she spent on the outskirts of town on the other side of the bay visiting her Dositheus (she would take him a wicker basket with a bottle of papaya wine and two chicken livers with raisins), Isidro would wash up at El Floridita.

"Let me have," the adipose figure would grunt as he seated himself, panting from the marathon it was for him to get from the entrance to the table, "that drink that carries the nickname of Mary Queen of England and of Ireland who did not hesitate to martyrize Protestants or execute her rival for the throne, plus an archbishop and another three hundred people . . ."

After his first salty sip, the gourmand would concentrate, not so much on the lobster in garlic sauce or the roast suckling pig with guava leaves swimming in cassava, as on the generously open décolletage of the young Zerlina of a waitress who, ever since his first visit, served him with wheedling chortles and pretended to understand his alcoholic riddles, which for her were boorish allusions to her bust and behind.

At the base of her cleavage, between the two nascent pearly spheres, bulging with bluish reflections à la Rubens, he could spy the diminutive slender lace of her brassiere. When the waitress came by to serve him, the fat man tried to breathe deeply to catch the aroma of her breasts, which he presumed to be tawny and musky, but the insistent odor of the shrimp's orange sauce blocked his way.

Isidro's purely electromagnetic conception of all phenomena had led him to practice radiesthesia: he was adept at the copper pendulum, which he swung over the unclothed bodies of patients, seeking the spot where it shifted or abruptly changed the direction of its rotation.

The pendulum also swung over, who could say why, his deepest fantasies. The fourth bloody mary, which by then he called for without circumlocutions, and the ever more confounding proximity of the waitress, led him without fail to his dominical nirvana: he saw her before him serving his cocktail and at the same time lying naked in his empty amphitheater. Using the pendulum, he explored without touching her trembling body.

When the rotations accelerated, he would place his right ear on her skin and listen to the blood rumble in her veins, and then he would continue roaming until he returned to the sound of her breathing, the whoosh of her lymphatic fluid, the creaking of her cartilage against the calcium in her bones: the entire infinitesimal swamp of life itself.

Thus he was able, without the lamentable impediment of culinary effluences, to sniff every bit of her, to breathe her in slowly, to assess her skin with his sense of smell, even the most humid and hidden parts, the very walls of her sex; he could hear the dull roar of the hairs of her pubis under the lobe of his own ear. And all this without anyone knowing, not even she, exposed as she was, unknowingly, to radiesthetic inspection – thanks to a small menstrual retardation.

Once he figured out who these prostration professionals were and why they had come, Firefly set to convincing himself of the gravity of his own illness. As a cover he devised a rigid catatonia and perfected it to such a degree that the doctors were faced with a wide-eyed wooden doll, gaze fixed on the zenith, a thread of transparent purple saliva drooling from his lips. Flies did not disturb him, nor did the handbell rung by the nun who dispensed the cane juice, which was so piercing and shrill it made even the moribund tremble.

In examinations of the parents and sister, which the experts undertook straight off, the pendulum's spin was sluggish, stumbling, knotted like the speech of a drunk. Such lethargy could be caused by anything, since magnetic disturbances often overwhelm sensitive bodies in the aftermath of a hurricane.

More revealing was the radiesthesic map of the aunts, the three of them wrapped in the same hypnosis, as if huddled under the red sealing wax of a single blanket. Very useful, it must be admitted, was the light interrogation that accompanied the auscultation, with responses obtained via screams in the ear, shakings, and slaps across the face.

They then turned to Firefly.

To the astonishment of the specialists, the copper cone spun normally up the length of that wooden body, but when it reached his heart the device jumped like a frightened rabbit: it stopped abruptly, remained still a few seconds, then began spinning crazily in the wrong direction. Clearly, the blood beat mightily and flowed in torrents through that pretend cadaver.

Isidro and Gator looked at each other, both suspecting the same thing. The herbalist turned and faced the garden, apparently intrigued by the plants; in reality he wanted to meditate on this enigma, which he intended to solve on the spot.

Then he swiveled back toward the bed of the petrified boy. Once more he scrutinized the stiff. "Precocious catalepsy," the experts declared in unison, though, smelling something fishy, they remained unconvinced.

Once the verdict had been pronounced, Isidro and Gator sat down on either side of the cot. The chubby one pulled the pendulum from the right-hand pocket of his trousers and suspended it in the air, observing it calmly, as if he wished to confirm the impeccable operation of the laws of gravity.

In his mind, Gator went over the various tonics or revivifying potions, all based on a French wine, Château des Mille Tremblements, mixed with rum and raw sugar, which he could insist the young patient, despite his inert, practically wooden state, drink through a cinnamon straw.

Isidro, while studying the pendulum's easy swing, peered at the melon-head with the astuteness of a caged bird, careful not to let him know he was being watched. Gator meanwhile was fascinated, or pretended to be, by the minuscule purple flowers that grew between the bricks, a practically extinct species that sprouted there alone due to the aseptic nature of the place. In reality, he was eyeing cataleptic Firefly from askance to see if he was breathing or not.

After these apparently incandescent inquiries, the two focused directly on scrutinizing this child overcome by the excesses of Morpheus. They understood instantly, and quickly exchanged glances out of the corners of their eyes like two accomplice snakes before a defenseless partridge, that something was not spinning smoothly in this strange case of *familial oneiromancy*.

The shining aunts were demanding they be "left in peace," that they "needed some shut-eye," believing they were washing clothes on the white stones of a large river during siesta hour, after a succulent codfish stew.

But let's go again to El Floridita, where the two maverick sawbones are now describing how they unmasked, thanks to a well-interpreted remark, the cataleptic's crude pretending. "From that triple swing of the inquisitor pendulum," the radiesthesist told the openmouthed waiters, including the operatic barmaid, indicating his guest the exemplary herbalist as witness, "had come *inescapable truths*." He underlined the words syllable by syllable. By then they had spiked Isidro's bloody potion three times over with angostura bitters and celery salt.

[37]

The waitress listened wide-eyed and artlessly dribbled across the tablecloth the soy sauce that was to dress a special wheat-germ steak (for the restaurant staff unnatural and evidently emetic) that a skillful cook had prepared for Gator. Before wiping it up, she gave a quick pull on the silk strap that sustained her décolletage.

"That's right," the herbalist continued, picking up the radiesthesist's long monologue as if they had been rehearsing their entire lives for this dramatic performance: the meeting of minds of two specialists puffed up by what the *Diario de la Marina* was calling their illustrious contribution to solving "the atrocity of the century." "That's right. No longer could we presume that this was simply the morbid reflex that quicksilver, when corrupted by the hurricane's magnetic disturbances, will project onto vulnerable bodies."

"No!" Isidro piled on, waving his right index finger in the air. "In a pause between ignoble snores, one of the Fates had assured them: Early in the morning, the family had carefully masked all the mirrors with black brocade."

On stretched a silence filled with suspense. He looked keenly at the slack-jawed waiters. Another sip. Meanwhile, Gator carried on, exalted by the fascination the duo evoked in the marinated listeners.

"The nocturnal bite of certain bats, as was well known by the

[38]

Ciboneys who at dawn would staunch the wounds with saffron flowers, leaves its victims groggy and exhausted. But in this case the insentient victims bore not the least sign of jugular perforation. What's more, knowing that those sucking sneaks always lie in wait, the family had not neglected the home's defenses, making ample prophylactic use of cloves of garlic.* Something, however, and this was our last resort, was affecting the lymphatic flow in each member of the family except the child, whose pendulum map was normal, though we did not have a clue as to what had caused the spell: the bite of a mosquito infected with a lethal virus, mass hypnosis . . . or a cataleptic potion."

"I was racking my brains," Isidro, after insisting on Worcestershire sauce for the next drink, "when suddenly one of the three narcissistic nasties opened her eyes and asked Firefly for nothing less than another cup of linden-flower tea as delicious as the one he'd made for her at home . . . That was when, like a bolt of lightning, I felt a spark of truth fly between two oppositely charged

* Thus works clairvoyance. The poor herbalist could not know that with these suspicions, even though later disproved, he was confirming Firefly's prediction when he heard the dispatch from the observatory and interpreted it as announcing an invasion of bats. Not even the seer himself understands his words – and I say this from my own experience. No science is capable of ordering *the abstruse language of vaticinations*.

poles: on the one hand, we had a ruse, yes, a catatonic ruse by the melon-head, who was the one with something to hide and who with that rictus of his rebuffed any possible interrogation; and on the other, we had the aunt's soothing and unknowingly revelatory request . . . Another linden-flower tea! Evidently, the crafty barracuda had given his family a sleeping potion, a diabolical concoction that he himself had not drunk, but whose effects – the scoundrel – he pretended to suffer."

"You criminal!" Isidro sputtered through clenched teeth. He pointed mercilessly at Firefly and hurled the pendulum to the floor amid a scattering of terrified nuns.

"You monster!" Gator echoed from the fountain, where his botanical ruminations had led him to the same conclusion at the very same time.

From the hospice wing across the courtyard, cupping their hands to their mouths and parting the mosquito nettings to reveal faces waxen or enraged, the lepers immediately began to howl "To the stocks!" though they had no clue who was being accused, or of what.

Have you seen the little kid in that Goya tapestry bobbing up and down on a tablecloth being shaken by four peasant women? Or those Chinese acrobats who bounce like beads on a taut string? Well, though it seems unbelievable, Firefly jumped just like that from the simple cot that sheltered him, no tablecloth, no taut string, as soon as he saw the outstretched, outsized arms of the radiesthesist and the herbalist coming at him like gyrating tentacles about to strangle him.

"That leap settled it." The obese one is now speaking without slides before a packed classroom. He waves the pendulum about like a pointer; nothing interrupts the sepulchral silence of the place but pencils and sighs; the devotees record with the former and concur with the latter the professor's all-encompassing evidence. "And it proved beyond any doubt that the energy contained in a 'catatonic simulation' can, via that hysterical conversion noted by Charcot, be transformed into 'agitation tremens.' There have been cases," he says, the mangy dog punctuating his sentences by rustling the beaded curtain, while a stink of potato soup wafts in from the kitchen, "of Teresian nuns, hardly acrobats, who went straight from ecstasis to compulsive flexion: drooling, their eyes glassy, they'd bend over backwards . . . until their heads touched their heels."

Let's leave the culpable extra-large cranium hanging in the air for a moment before he completes his fall. A moment to analyze the situation, to unravel if possible the Gordian knot of this "familicidal" personality, as the *Diario de la Marina* put it in their apt headline, yet "vulnerable, even fragile, ever affectionate, at times exemplary."

Whoever is innocent, or believes himself to be, defends himself. Whoever retains some trace of purity, a surviving smidgen of his original decency, answers the accusations. But he who is wholly guilty, or who suspects as much, can do nothing but remain silent, hide his face, dodge insults, flee.

The poor melon-head figures his error is indelible and he is lost for good; that is why he leaps the way he leaps. Reproof and self-disgust are what give rise to his bounding energy. Nothing else. It is the "urgent, urgent" need (he repeats the word to himself) to become somebody else that explains his sudden ability to jump.

So much so that he can visualize his own body hanging there. And he feels it so sullied and blameworthy that it has become no more than a charcoal silhouette, a dirty rag, a useless black burden. Better to let himself fall, allow himself to plummet as if he were still astride that fecal cistern. Allow himself to slide toward his mother, run into her open arms, hear her voice next to his ear: "It's all over now, it's all over now."

He lands back on the cot as the accuser and his pal, who is brandishing a bunch of purple plants, followed by several breathless and blood-curdling nuns, close in on their prey. Purulent fingers point at him once again: "Make him pay for his crime! The devilish monster! He tried to poison his own family!"

The hairless Chinaman bounces like a doll stuffed with sawdust. Weak. Utterly without strength. And the tiny bit that remains he draws on to run.

He crossed the courtyard diagonally. The accusing shouts of the lepers fell on him like a rain of hot stones and ash through which he barely managed to move; a very familiar paralysis began to take hold of him, like tetanus rising up from his feet. Urging himself on, he tried to reach the tiled door but felt his legs refuse. Then he tried to scream. As in a dream, he opened his mouth, sent air rushing from his throat, from his chest, from his belly. He pushed hard. Nothing came out.

It seemed to him undeniable that his body had become superfluous, a useless excess, morbid, better eliminated so the world could recover its equilibrium, its original harmony. It was as if something or someone were urgently demanding his exclusion, his eradication in the pursuit of cleanliness and an ideal of order. He imagined the peevish gesture of an immaculate muscled hand, flicking from some untainted marble a disgusting insect, a larva, a crazy man's spittle, something abject yet visible, a focal point attracting everyone's gaze like a magnet: that which must be extirpated.

From the lepers' wing, clutching it as best she could with her two bleeding stumps, an old woman with a nose devoured by cankers tossed a basin at him, rubber enema hose and all, filled with sour wastewater that spattered him and provoked an irrepressible desire to throw up. Then another of the decayed women who had seen it all raced to her bed, bawling insults or mocking scorn in a mousy singsong, and quickly returned with a rotten mango, which she also threw at him.

Fortunately, Firefly had by then crossed the threshold and was in the front yard of the hospice. At the last moment, he turned to look back at the ward that held the catatonics. He had the fleeting impression that his sister was waking up and glancing around uneasily, looking for him.

Little by little, the city had begun to recover from the storm. Storekeepers, between sobs, totted up their losses.

He was in the street. It was morning. From a nearby market came the calls of fishermen; pushcart wheels squealed on the paving stones. Harried planters crowded around a slaver. They tasted the sweat of the black women, bargained, then packed them into carts and carried them off to distant sugar mills to be deposited in malodorous barracks. Also reaching him in the little square, like stampedes of color, were beams from the rising sun reflected off the awnings that covered the kiosks: yellow canvases that returned the light or spread it across the limestone façades, on pyramids of mammee or pineapple. In the middle of one golden stall, the breeze undid little piles of purple and red powders for offerings.

Surrounded by the throng, he felt the useless dross of his body, the sensation that he was dragging about a stain or a burden from which he could not free himself. Guilt surrounded him like an opaque aura; an invisible leprosy devoured his skin. He was hungry and thirsty. He wanted someone to play with. To see his sister. He recalled his father's footsteps in the corridor of the house, the early clattering of his mother in the kitchen, the owl that from the garden ceiba tree awakened him each night, the far-off strumming of guitars, the misplaced steps of singing drunks. He yearned for a long deep sleep. He wanted to die and be born again, to return to the state that precedes birth and succeeds death. He wanted to de-exist. To become somebody else.

He found himself lost among the vendors in the little square, amid a tumult of shoppers, passersby, fleeting nuns, cabin boys, leering quadroons, pickpockets, card sharks, knife-sharpeners, witch doctors, medical astrologists, herbalists, swindlers, and slaves. He knew not where to go or what to do. One thing he did know for sure: Never again would he have a home or a family, a place of origin or repose. Flight had cut off his roots, thrust him into an exile with no return. Although he had only just left them, his mother's lap, his sister's voice, a bed covered in gifts, and, upon rising, the smell of bread with salted oil and a mug of coffee, it all seemed very distant, like a fuzzy recollection, almost like a dream.

He was weak, trembling, his skin mortuary pallor. He felt someone was about to grab him by the scruff of the neck like a cat and hoist him up into the void, then let him fall from on high and smash against the paving stones, just to watch the bits of his brain and blood bounce.

He huddled against a marble fountain with four dolphins, whose cool jets he tried to reach. Beggars pleaded for crumbs and even doubloons from the calash drivers done up in frock coats and bowler hats; a Manila shawl slipped off the shoulders of a Creole lady and fell into a pile of horse manure.

An elderly black woman passing by, dressed neatly in white linen with a silk turban, picked poor Firefly up. She was wearing necklaces, earrings, and bracelets made of tiny shells, also white, which, when she hoisted him higher to caress his head, rang in his ear like the rattles of his infancy, like the maternal murmur.

"I cannot care for you, my son," she whispered with regret while smoothing his hair with her hands, "because I already have many with what God has given me, and they are waiting at home. But I will take you to a very big and very pretty house with ceiling fans and a refrigerator and everything, where a white woman, kind and clean as only she can be, will give you a little glass of *crème de vie*."

Lack of air

"Milk," answered Munificence. "Condensed milk. Two cups."

"What else?" Firefly asked, licking his lips.

"Rum. Three tablespoons of rum. And two eggs, beaten. Just the yolks. You save the whites for meringue."

"It'll make you strong."

"Now, to work. Before bed you'll get a big bowl of soup with a slice of bread and a bit of bacon. Porridge in the morning. But we've got a lot to do. More?"

"I can't, my head's spinning."

Munificence was sitting with her back against a white stone fireplace, a useless holdover from the turn-of-the-century colonial style that for no reason but overblown pretentiousness had filled the island's stifling living rooms with cloying volutes and ornate window frames. Two large windows, always open, failed to cool the moth-eaten stacks of notaries' folders stuck in transit to or from the offices on the upper floor; the shelves were all overflowing with pasteboard notebooks, each threaded by a red marker ribbon, offered up to spiderwebs and dust.

During the end-of-year drought they called winter, they would close the book cabinets and fill the fireplace with mahogany logs or some sort of aromatic fresh-cut wood that never quite burned and would become a favorite haunt of rats fat as hutia tree rodents, bulimic beasts that went on from that woodpile to lay claim to everything devourable until the next dry season when the decorative mahogany logs would be replaced and the rodents would start in all over again.

Munificence was enormously tall, a pole for knocking cats off the roof. Behind her back, the "girls" – as she called the innocents forgotten or confined by their parents in the big charity house adjoining the offices – called her "the flaming giraffe," and to gratify her in public they never failed to compare her height to her generosity.

The shoes she wore made her even taller, as did the taffeta suit with vertical white stripes and the faded gardenia pinned high up on her blond hair, which was always braided Venetian style, fashioned into a cylindrical roll and drenched in hair spray: No rebellious wisp could ever break free.

The girls frolicked in spirals around Munificence, playing hand games, pinching each other, stifling sudden fears and giggles; they were big butterflies, sumptuous and mischievous, or red-headed squirrels shaking off the frost after an interminable hibernation.

"Is this your house?" Firefly asked Munificence, handing back the mug.

"No," the tower replied, "I just come to these offices to keep an eye on things. A fire would be the end of it all, there's so much paper. My house is in the back on the other side of the yard. It's the charity home where I take care of these angels."

Little by little, in the days that followed, Firefly discovered the connections between these two places and the rules that governed each, though he was never sure he grasped their true meaning.

The office building's big three-bolt door and two large windows faced the street. The ground floor was just a cemetery for unfulfilled contracts, invalid legal papers, and files gnawed by the rats. A pointlessly vast staircase led to a diminutive mezzanine, then on to the second floor, where the city's shadiest notaries had set up shop. A moth-eaten recamier, used as a depository for old dockets in one of the offices, became Firefly's nightly resting place.

The purple shadow of a large ceiba tree cooled the office-building yard and spread over the course of the day from a gold-fish pond, whose care was immediately given over to Firefly, to a pair of wrought-iron gates. Beyond one of them, in the distance, lay a basket workshop populated by tattered and raucous Gypsies who never paused in their wicker-weaving or their singing; the other gate led to the dormitory, a structure similar to the office building and just as dilapidated and decayed but lacking windows and its own exit to the street. There, Munificence's pupils kept their bedrooms swept clean and had their sewing workshop, the handful of Singers so well-oiled they made practically no sound; during working hours one could hear the chapter being read out by the reader of the day.

A seminarian with very fine whiskers dusted the minuscule gold-and-red chapel every Sunday.

To reach the street on their way to school, the girls raced impetuously through the first floor of the offices, zigzagging around the furniture buried in paper: "A sip of vinegar," Munificence told them about that bit, "which you'll have to endure."

Not knowing exactly why, Firefly began spying on the pupils, though he could only devote himself to that solitary pleasure after six in the afternoon. Once he was old enough, the melon-head spent his days in frenetic, breathless races between the offices and the corner store, a Mozarabic tray in hand bearing stained and tottering little glasses of coffee with condensed milk, croissants, pastries dripping with clear syrup, mille-feuilles, sacred-heart cakes, Morón cookies, and candied guava, brilliantly red like garnet, crowned with little squares of fresh cheese.

He also went for tobacco and stamps, Dutch quarto paper, envelopes, change, the afternoon papers; he cleaned the offices redolent with ink, picked up the trash, swept the shelves with an ostrich-feather duster, and using two legal documents even shined the shoes of the scriveners who would stop by their cubicles always in the morning and always in a hurry to consult certain records and tear up others, erase names and numbers or change them for what they had scribbled on little slips of paper, which they would simply paste over the old ones.

Munificence set him up in the document depot so that he might make something of himself and thus be saved from hunger, orphanage, plague, alcohol, and women.

He received considerable tips, for sure, but much more in the way of taunts and abuse. The lawyers with their black leather briefcases did not hesitate to reproach him with a slap across the cheek for coffee grown cold along the way, for a wormy piece of fruit, or even for lack of deference in the way he was obliged to address them.

Once they had left for the day, and Munificence had slid the three bolts closed, he would watch the swimming goldfish, hide his face, and cry.

Among the frisky girls, Firefly quickly zeroed in on one, plumper and whiter than the rest, with red hair and large violet eyes. She smelled terrific: of powdered lavender and mothballs.

He saw her again early one morning in her school uniform: white blouse, Prussian blue skirt with a ribbon at the hem, high patent leather shoes, and a stack of rag-paper notebooks cinched to her back; she held the straps taut with her thumbs in front of her breasts. Despite the load, she walked erect, looking straight ahead, like an Indian from the highlands with a cargo of coca leaves.

Firefly raced to the front room for a closer look; she was sliding open the bolts on the wooden door. Her fragrance wafted toward him, not lavender now but ground-bee honey, which is sweet and dark and heals all, but whose wax can block your ears and make you deaf.

She had her red hair pulled back and tied at the neck with a strip of mauve felt; gray stockings, like a nun's, clung to her legs. Now that he had her so close, the scent of lavender returned like the first time, and he understood that *he loved her for her aromas.*

Munificence's other pupils were just as pretty, and their big teeth and clean unadorned ears even reminded him of his aunts, but none of them smelled like her. Munificence did once, when she gave him the *crème de vie*.

Firefly approached and timidly touched the backpack of notebooks. "What's your name?"

"Ada," the redhead answered grumpily, as if she were being pestered by a buzzing insect.

"Hada?" the melon-head considered. "That's not the name of a real person, it's a storybook character."

"And what's your name?" the squirrel retorted before closing the door in his face.

"Firefly."

"Firefly?" she asked with a smirk from the sidewalk. "That's not the name of a real person, it's a bug."

The next day a loud ruckus startled him.

The yelling from deep within the charity house came closer, imprecations, insults, and threats which Firefly could not make out but which echoed around the yard, causing the quintessentially quarrelsome and meddlesome notaries to lean out the windows and even to empty an ashtray full of disgusting butts onto the caterwauling women, and then bang it in a conga rhythm on the blue windowsill.

Munificence had taken hold of one of the youngest and weakest students, a girl in uniform but strangely barefoot. She had her by the arms, as if she were a rabid beast about to bite.

The prisoner squirmed, kicked every which way, bit at her executioner's wrists to try and wriggle free.

Was she a rebellious student, too young for the charity's stern rules? What Firefly saw on closer viewing left him baffled: She was more like an old woman, wrinkled and scrawny, disguised as a pupil. Or the opposite: a withered and pasty infant, prematurely devastated by scurvy or nerves. Her shiny hair was streaked with gray, or maybe excessively blond, washed with chamomile or the peroxide they use as a disinfectant.

"You're expelled!" screamed Munificence, beside herself and mortified. "Expelled!"

Taking as witnesses the students who had followed her from the charity house with their wicker hoops, embroidery needles, and balls of yarn, plus the big-shot lawyers, exhilarated by the melee, who had come down to the landing on the stairs, and Firefly himself, she accused: "She's bedeviled! She's cursed! They caught her in the chapel praying backwards. Under her pillow they found a copper stone, a white-and-maroon necklace, and two seashells. The witch!"

She managed to haul her to the front door.

Then, like a big uncoordinated doll, her face white with egg-shell powder or rage, she threw the girl into the street with all her strength.

"You'll see," the platinum girl screamed from the sidewalk, expending the last of her energy in a death rattle. "You'll see how I take revenge. I leave it all in God's hands."

And she limped off.

Munificence came back inside. She closed the door and shrugged.

He slept curled up on the recamier, elbows touching knees. In the morning, he would straighten up his bedding of dockets of irreconcilable cases, obtuse demands, or specious suits against unknowns, the trials of which were periodically postponed and for that reason were not to be filed away. Before bed, he would calmly stack the most crumpled documents at the foot of the sofa; the softest ones, those that had been fingered for years and had turned silky like tobacco leaves, made a good pillow. Amid the querulous papers he always fell right to sleep, protected by their cane fibers, by their night of ink. He dreamed about hefty sealing-wax stamps, a squirrel devouring nuts, and also an enormous white wooden house by the sea. Gulls knocked against the windowpanes; the nighttime coast was full of fireflies lighting up the grass with their phosphorescent lamps. Someone, perhaps his sister, told him something about that pulsating green, something he could not understand. He yelled at her to explain. Then he would awaken soaked in sweat, crying. One night he peed on the recamier.

That imperial couch lay on the creaky floorboards beside the window of a cramped office. From there he could look out at the yard, the ceiba tree and its nocturnal owls, the first rays of sun reflected off the pond, maybe the red stain of a fish, the early-morning departure of the pupils and their punctual return at dawn as the six raucous bells of the cathedral rang out.

Despite his vigilance, it was not sight but sound one rainy morning that alerted him to the nearness of Ada: the toes and heels of the high patent leather shoes tapping across the moist paving stones of the yard. He leaped from the recamier. He rubbed his eyes hard to reassure himself he was not dreaming. No, it was she. From the window he saw her walk toward the offices, indifferent to the rain, erect, proud, gazing at the top of the ceiba as if she were looking for a bird, with that way of angling her shoulders before turning, before tilting the rest of her body and circling the pool, as if she were announcing her trajectory, her destiny.

She stopped abruptly. Her gaze followed the ephemeral rings traced by the fish; she moistened the tips of her fingers in the cool water and dried them on her blue skirt. She continued on to the front room, thumbs looped in the straps.

Firefly waited a moment. He slept fully dressed, so he smoothed his clothes with his hands, and his hair too, before going after her. He bounded down the staircase, skipping steps like someone possessed.

"Ada," he said panting, now by the door, "Ada . . ."

"What can I do for you?" And she shook her red hair, which today she wore loose and turned up at the ends like a cabin boy.

"I've got something to tell you . . ."

"I've no time."

Firefly never knew why what came to mind in that moment, as if he were looking at a photograph, was the explanation Munificence gave him one day about the heart and the blood. He understood there and then the blue trembling he could see in the veins of his arms. That was all he knew of the human body, although at night he would rub himself still clothed against the silk of the recamier, an exercise that never went beyond tedium, never assuaged his fear or even revealed why he felt the urge to do it.

Yet he knew that this was what he wanted to talk to her about: the fragility of the body, that miracle. If the heart stops, death comes. That was why he did not want Ada to sleep, ever, so that her heart would never forget to beat.

"Ada, I want to tell you something about the heart."

"Leave me alone," the red giant responded. "I've already heard plenty of nonsense."

"Ada . . . your laces . . ."

The very same angel that had guided him down the cistern and out of the hospital now blew these words his way.

"The laces of your right shoe."

She did no more than stick out her foot and gaze at the mezzanine windowpanes while Firefly kneeled down and tied the laces in a double bow with such tender care it could have been her heart he was touching instead of her shoes. Then he rested the palm of his right hand on the patent leather toe, as if he hoped his sweat would cloud its shine.

Ada pulled her foot back. She turned away. She walked on to the door and slid open the bolts.

Firefly remained doubled over, looking at his own dirty shoes wrinkled like two old skins, his darned socks, the perfect geometry of the joins between the floor tiles, and then the door by which Ada had gone out, the open bolts that perhaps still retained the warmth of her white hands.

He wanted to race after her, to find another pretext to touch her. But a sudden pain caught him in the middle of his chest, a vicious lack of air. He heard whistling when he breathed, felt he was suffocating. It was obvious his heart was about to give out. To recover, he had once been told, he needed a bowl of hot soup made from the turkey buzzard that soars so high. But for the moment all he had was choking, hacking, lack of air. Ada was air. He unbuttoned his shirt. Something told him not to move, to try to breathe deeply and slowly, to think of something else.

It was useless. Ada was air. And she was far away.

He was about to keel over and split his head on the tiles, when he heard the sudden squeal of the hinges.

He looked up. Through the gap in the half-open door Ada's head appeared, looking for him.

"Thanks," the redhead shouted.

And she slammed the door shut.

It was morning. Yet it seemed to him that the day was ending, that the light was retreating and abandoning the furniture, the room, every little thing bit by bit. He understood then that what he lacked was not air or a clear view of things or Ada's body. The something missing was much more vast and obscure, something neither close at hand nor far away, rather running parallel. The work of doing without was incessant: gnawing, gnawing. The nocturnal rumbling of rats terrified by the flood after the hurricane. Hardworking rats, devouring the wood in the fireplace.

He recalled the house by the sea, heard the roar of the waves, saw a great lamp of tarnished copper swinging in the center of the room; the luminous green of the fireflies went dark. Now, lack flooded everything. Even Ada's body. It gnawed at everything, contaminated everything. It soiled every existing thing with its inanity.

"Firefly! Firefly dear!"

From the mezzanine, Munificence was calling him.

A STABLE THOUGHT BETWEEN
TWO BOUTS OF LUNACY

The days went by, each identical to the one before, in gloomy treks for café con leche and candied guava. Identical, but not for him. He kept up his nighttime vigil, rubbing his sex against the silk, and his ridiculous daytime frenzy. But he was no longer his old self, rather somebody else, somebody plagued by doubts. Not about Ada's feelings, or the possibility he might be the victim of a sick joke, or what lay behind the notaries' despotic abuse; no, rather doubts about the munificence of Munificence, for example, about whether everything came down to its appearance or its reality.

So he took up spying, but not like before. He no longer knew what to spy on, or whom. For days on end, throughout the interminable rainy season, in the endless owl-filled nights.

Until one evening by the fishpond, when the lamps were going out, he saw that one second-floor notary office remained lit. He could make out, yes it was she, Munificence's silhouette behind a tulle curtain, then Ada's looking inhibited, timid. And then those of two men, one short and stout, likely in shirt and tie, the other taller and gawky, briefcase in hand.

No doubt about it: It was them.

But why were they here?

As powerfully as he had needed air, he sensed he was about to find out. Up to that moment he had lived in the clouds, without happiness but also without worry. He cared more now about learning the truth than about breathing: What were they doing here, the accusers who had unmasked his make-believe at the hospital?

Several thoughts battered him, each of them unbearable.

Isidro and Gator, if indeed it was them, had come for him. They would gag him and haul him off to a dungeon and put him on bread and water for the rest of his life. They would hand him over to the lepers so they could spit on him and rub their purulent stumps in his face. They would auction him off as a child slave, naked in the market, covered in sores; a sugar baron would buy him, just to whip him.

Maybe the maniacal fat guy was looking for fresh dupes for the pendulum demonstrations in the darkness of his amphitheater. He did not really understand what that was all about, but in his heart he knew it was something devious, unspeakable.

Like a feverish shudder came the thought that they might take Ada's body away from him, that over it they would dangle the morbid rotations of the copper cone with its mortuary shine and its iridescent gyrating like a sick lightning bug.

He wondered how they had discovered him, tracked him down, why his parents had not come, and who had brought the redhead into it. Or perhaps – and this possibility rocked him with the violence of vomiting – it was she who had tipped off the inquisitors.

What was the truth? What was Munificence's real work? Could it all be a simple coincidence, a joke, an entertainment of *gods with nothing to do*, something akin to when two children from the same family die at the same moment in different places? The two bigwigs – he continued to feed this fond hope – might have simply dropped by for a visit, or on some complicated secret errand with the notaries. There was nothing to fear. Ada's presence was just another coincidence. She would soon leave, discreetly. And so would the interlopers. The lamp would go out. He would hear the piercing squeal of the door closing, Munificence's footsteps heading off to the charity house.

Everything would return to its stifled monotony, smooth and unbroken, like a flat polished surface; everything would again occur at its predetermined hour: the punctual departure of the pupils, the morning sun on the ceiba tree, the fish darting amid the mossy rocks, the voices of the busy weavers from the basket workshop, the horn of a car in the street, the wind, the wind . . .

But it was not to be. The lamp remained lit. A few interminable minutes passed. Suddenly the visitors stood up together, seemingly compelled by something. They began to wave their arms about as if they were tossing a rag doll or a stinking stuffed animal that Firefly thought he saw somersaulting in the air. The same thoughts from before came rushing back, now twisted or deformed, in fragments. He sensed they were speaking about him. He had no idea why now again he saw the white wooden house by the sea, abandoned this time, devoured by the salt air, invaded by sand; a door on the left bore a wooden sign with what once must have been gilt letters: THE PAVILION.

Another thought suddenly accosted him, this one concise and urgent like an order. He ran to the charity house, crept into the kitchen, and headed toward the yellow cupboard where he knew Munificence hid the *crème*, and as if wanting to accumulate transgressions (nothing was more forbidden to him than entering the pupils' lodgings), he forced it open with a swift kick. In one long draft, he slugged back all that was left in the bottle.

He stared, contemplating the tall, empty, misshapen bottle, dull as if it had donned a coat of plaster, quivering alongside a gray crock also blanched, the bottle drained of everything, in the grip of something he knew all too well: fear.

He scrutinized the mustard yellow of the cabinet, the assortment of painted birds fluttering around fruit, the bouquet of golden flowers.

He felt the alcohol running through his veins, making its way out from the center, a fire blossoming inside his body; the diminutive red petals were a rain shower falling slowly over a city to set it aflame, to calm it down.

The objects on the table, the bottle and the crock, seemed less frightened, as if they had regained the security of the hand that had molded them, the calm of the potter's wheel from which they had emerged, the certainty of a day guided by the parabola of the sun. They seemed to be filling up, not with texture or color but with themselves, their own voices, or the muted echo of their being. He watched them now, face-to-face, as they took on their own essence, coincided with their own shapes, teemed with themselves.

He breathed deeply, free of distress. Fresh air, bluish, pure. The rhythm of his breathing was a far-off sea. The oxygen flowed through him and purified him bit by bit, even his fingernails and hair, every inch of his skin.

That was it, composure: an intermission between two crises, a stable thought between two bouts of lunacy.

He returned to the patio with what he thought was a confident step. He did not know how much time he had spent contemplating the bottle and the crock, observing the slow yellowing of the plaster that covered them, the appearance of ephemeral cracks. Though in the time others keep, it seemed to him, it had all happened very quickly.

The lamp in the office was still on, the window a yellow rectangle cut from the purple night. The four silhouettes remained frozen in the position in which he had left them, no gestures, no movement.

All of a sudden, with the abruptness of a swat, Munificence shattered the immobility of that wax museum. She had thrown something in Gator's face; something had struck him, wounded him, perhaps a glass. The herbalist put his hands to his face, to his mouth, as if trying to staunch the blood. Isidro approached with what looked like a handkerchief. Then they rushed out. Gator, one hand still pressed to his mouth, hung on to the fat man's arm with the other.

Ada and Munificence sat down across from each other, the tutor in a higher chair, where she looked to be in charge.

Firefly, liberated by the departure of the visitors, ran to the offices. He panted up the staircase. He knocked on the office door. No answer. Cautiously, slowly, he pushed it open. He peeked inside.

"Have the men gone?" he asked, flushed, bathed in a sudden sweat.

"The men?" Munificence asked back, surprised. "What men? No man has come here. Besides," and she slayed him with a reproachful look, "you're drunk. Utterly, completely drunk."

And she shook him by the shoulders to bring him back to his senses.

He does not know what happened next. Nor where he spent the night. He awoke back in the yard. His hair was wet. To sober him up, someone had dunked his head in the fishpond. He guessed the time by the height of the sun and the noise of typewriters in the offices: twelve noon.

The owl took off from the top of the ceiba tree and rose

vertically, wings spread, white symmetry in the whitened midday sky, and after several ever-expanding circles took refuge in its daytime hideout, the bell tower of the cathedral.

Amid damp green-and-yellow pyramids of freshly woven baskets, the Gypsies were cooking their lunch of dense phyllo pastries stuffed with olives.

Had he dreamed it all, like the white wooden house by the sea, like the phosphorescence of the lightning bugs above the sand? Was it simply delirium, a trumped-up story both gratuitous and meticulous, contrived by drink? Or were they fooling him again, making fun of him, callously playing with his frailty? But why?

He decided to search on the sly for some clue, some trace, convinced that if the visitors had been real they must have left a mark. Likely more than one, since the assault he half saw had seemed so real.

He perceived – but it was immaterial, indemonstrable – the dark emanation of the events like the tenuous impalpable shadow that remains in a room after a crime and which no one can point to but some people find unbearable.

Quietly he climbed the stairs to the office illuminated the night before. He was welcomed, as usual, by a fat-cheeked lawyer wearing blue-tinted bifocals and a gold watch chain, holding his head in his hands, either the victim of a migraine or lost in the twists and turns of some extortion.

"A café con leche really hot and a ham-and-cheese sandwich," the man yelled at once. And he angrily pounded a yellowed document with a sealing-wax stamp, as if he meant to punch a hole right through it.

Firefly did not obey the order; on the contrary, he advanced a few steps toward the center of the office, observing everything, scrutinizing each object, searching for a sheaf of papers out of place, a fold in the rug, a sliver of glass. There was nothing.

"Why aren't you on your way?" the lawyer scolded. "Are you in limbo or what the hell's wrong with you?" Then suddenly changing his tone, he chuckled. "Ah, I forgot. My mind's somewhere else."

He held out a one-peso note.

Firefly left the office. His eyes scoured the floor. He heard them summoning him with a bell and with shouts from the other offices. But he paid no heed; he did not even go for the litigator's order.

He was looking for a sign. More: for proof of his sanity.

Repeatedly, he went up and down the stairs. He combed the mezzanine. He returned, under the pretext that they had no change, to the scene where it all supposedly occurred. Nothing. And yet . . .

Disheartened and exhausted, he was about to give up the search and accept it was just alcohol playing tricks or mind-games spun by his imagination. He was ready to sink to the floor in tears, ready to head back to the yellow cupboard, when amid the chaos of the threadbare furniture on the first floor, on the leather of an easy chair people had to brush past to get to the door, he found, still fresh, no older than a night, *a trickle of blood.*

Now everything seemed linked, definitive: overlapping causes connected to consequences by indestructible bonds, like animals devouring and regurgitating one another from now until the ultimate extinction. Everything was crystal clear. Yet by late afternoon doubts accosted again him. Maybe it had been he himself, drunk, who had been wounded? Maybe the blood was old? With the same minute care with which he had scrutinized the office, he inspected his body in the mirror, millimeter by millimeter, an archaeologist of his own skin.

Nothing.

The following day he took to drink once more.

And the day after that.

At first he fixed the yellow cupboard so Munificence would not notice the break-in, and he doctored the *crème*, reducing its alchemy with equal measures of harsh rum and condensed milk, but found it insipid and repugnant and stopped straightaway. Then, with his morning coffee he would search the pantry for bottles of beer he could hide among the dockets and then sip bit by bit in furtive paper cups between his hurried and irritating errands.

At six in the afternoon, when the notaries abandoned their cubicles, he would leisurely take the last warm sips and begin to ruminate on Ada and the interloping quacks. Paper cup in hand, he would go down into the yard and stand next to the fishpond by the gate that led to the basket workshop. He would watch the Gypsies weave in silence, eat standing up, and on Sundays and after baptisms (they were believers and prolific) sing and dance, lifting their colorful ruffled skirts, clapping their hands, and stamping their heels. He watched them through the wrought iron, their arms raised very high to sketch arabesques, their bodies stretching and twisting as if they yearned to catch fire. Everything they did seemed to be one big party, cante jondo, heralds of Ada, rum, deep cool breaths that reached the bottom of his lungs, imminence of definitive departure, the red and gold of the waving skirts, the white of the baggy sleeves, the silver of the Moorish bracelets. And the gravelly voice, the voice of rum, and the arms reaching up so the hands could scribble on the sky.

Everything was a party. Yet in those inaccessible songs, in the scratchy voices worn by alcohol and the waning light of afternoon, he thought he heard something from his childhood, from the time when people nailed the doors shut to keep out the screams of the spirits: the innocent children, throats slit by the Inquisition, back with their interminable wailing, their voices rent but recognizable. For the voice is the only thing that remains intact after death.

Haven't you ever seen a bat smoke?

Firefly tried to forget that inopportune visit or chalk it up to his imagination or to drink. Now he could enter and leave his office hideaway whenever he wished: He had his own key and was in charge of the door bolts. His voice was still high-pitched like a bamboo flute, but rubbing his sex against the silk of the recamier now shook him from tip to toe and did not end dry like before. Upon rising, he would pull a page from one of the files, crumple it in his hand, and wipe up the white stain.

Of the outside world, he was now familiar with Plaza del Vapor, the rooming houses painted indigo, mustard, and green under the royal poincianas with their tentacle roots. He knew a bird shop where an old man in thick glasses trained canaries and the window of a crippled woman who painted piggy banks. He could also distinguish the aromas of a Chinese restaurant, of the talcum women wore, and of fresh-cut wood from a sawmill, which was his favorite – it was like sharpening a pencil. He knew where they sold oysters in little cups, where there was a blue lamp, always lit, shining on women who never sat down.

He spoke with no one, never set foot in a store, never stayed out after sundown, not even on Sunday. He had only one set of clothes, which he washed at night. If he had a beer, he drank it alone.

One Sunday he returned from the harbor. He had seen an Italian ship festooned with bunting for a party on board. Women in tight-fitting white silk gowns and peacock-feathered hats had been tossing paper streamers in the air and flinging empty champagne bottles off the stern. Bursts of laughter reached all the way to the park, where Sunday strollers reveled in the celebration.

He opened the big door, passed the threadbare furniture, shoved aside a stool with his foot, took the stairs to the mezzanine and on up to the second floor. His mind was not on his whereabouts, rather on the words he had heard from the ship. A woman dressed to the nines had leaned over the first-class rail and, between giggles, yelled, *"I'm not expecting anyone, but I'm convinced someone is going to come!"*

He was about to enter the moth heaven that was his room,

when he saw pressed against an office door, standing stock-still, a figure he could not make out in the darkness of the hallway. Someone was peeking through a keyhole or glued to the wood listening, apparently not even breathing, eavesdropping on what was occurring inside.

He approached silently. No doubt about it. It was she, Ada, so fascinated by what she was hearing that she did not even notice his presence, his nearness. When he reached her the redhead gave a start and covered her mouth. Having stifled her cry, she put a finger to her lips, opening wide those purple eyes in which Firefly thought he could see himself acknowledged, perhaps reflected, as in a minuscule and convex ship's mirror.

"Who is it?" the melon-head asked straight off in a whisper, as if the snooping had rekindled a long-standing complicity of which this chance meeting was but an astute step, minutely plotted.

She moved close, her lips to his ear. Her mothball-and-violets perfume, the rhythm of her breathing, the warmth of her breath against the lobe of his ear all shook him with the same intensity as the fear or desire that made him tremble when he rubbed himself against the silk or the words he had overheard coming from the ship.

"It's them," the redhead murmured, as if their identities went without saying. "Them again."

Firefly's right hand went to his throat, his breath caught short. "The same ones? Are you sure?"

"Yup. Greaseball and Boots from his own skin."

"The healers . . . Isidro and Gator, those are their names . . ."

"Them . . ."

"So . . . how come?"

Ada touched one of her index fingers to the other in a rapid indication of a bridge, a contact, an electrical charge, something going on between the peroxide giraffe and the odious men.

Inside, the conversation stopped.

Firefly was about to say, "Let's get out of here," when the door flew open.

The spied-upon trio came into view. They were rigid, flushed with contained rage. In the middle reigned Munificence, her Venetian tower in full erection, an emblem of unwavering determination. On either side, like two merciless Cerberuses awaiting the order to kill, were Fatso (his alcoholism evident in the pendular oscillation of his gelatinous body and in the incandescence of his beady eyes, now tinged orange like a vulture's behind those heavy lenses) and bearded Gator, who brandished a decoction like an avenging dagger in his raised right hand, his face frozen in an infanticidal smirk.

From these offended souls emanated a reproving, practically

[78]

mucilaginous silence that stuck to the skin, that befouled, and that – Firefly felt it immediately – also enveloped the redhead, trapping the two of them in a single net of disgust.

It was Munificence who spoke up, without raising her voice, her teeth clenched tight enough to squeak.

"I knew it," she spit out each syllable, the words like hissing blow-darts sent to punch holes in them. A moment of silence, then, "What a disgrace my life is! What a disgrace!"

She leapt upon the defenseless redhead as if on a bloodied prey, seizing her in the blink of an eye by both shoulders. Quickly she covered her mouth and hauled her the length of the hall and down the stairs.

Firefly thought he heard Ada's sobs, then realized he was alone with the two henchmen. What surprised him most, however, was not the suddenness of his abandonment but the inexplicable reaction of the visitors: They looked at each other, as astounded as the melon-head himself . . . and they burst out laughing!

"So, now we're grown up, little man!" Gator fired at him derisively while opening the door wide and stepping aside, extending his hand toward the interior of the office in a gesture of invitation.

"Come in, young gentleman, come in," Isidro added in the same tone. "As you can see, there is still plenty left for a surprise guest."

On the desk, with no more utensils than two baccarat goblets, a kitchen knife, a stack of paper plates and another of paper napkins, they had laid out a veritable cold banquet. The chicken salad had stained the green leather that covered the desktop. Plunged into a meatball minus a bite was a little red plastic fork.

"Now you've got the keys just like the man of the house . . ."

Firefly wondered how and from whom Gator had learned that detail.

"At the least," the reptile continued, "you, sir, ought to smoke a good cigar, don't you think?"

"And sure enough," Isidro took up the lead voice, "here's one of the finest Romeo y Julietas."

He broke into a sebaceous giggle.

Gator struck a match and lit the Havana himself, inhaling hard.

"Suck in that smoke!" he ordered. "You've got too much on your mind."

A snigger.

Firefly was standing next to the desk. He tried with all his strength to say, "I don't want to." But not a word emerged.

He had no idea why he looked at his feet. They were firmly on the ground, the laces well tied. He thought he heard the tinkling of the cut glass hanging from the dusty old lamp, as happened whenever there was a lot of wind or when disoriented birds, fleeing the fumigated warehouses of the port, found their way inside.

Unaware how much time had passed, he heard in a dream or echoing over a loudspeaker the inquisitor's stentorian voice: "Here is your cigar."

Firefly shook his head.

Then the man with scaly skin and bloodshot eyes, loosening his tie and his fly at the same time, as if an urgent need had overcome him, swayed into the office next door and disappeared.

He returned wielding another cigar, this one twisted and greenish. Closing his zipper, he came toward Firefly, his gaze fixed on something nonexistent but vile, like a liquor stain or a yellow smear.

The poor melon-head watched him approach and hid his sweaty hands in his pockets. His knees were trembling and he understood at once that he would not be able to move or speak.

"If you don't want that one," Gator ordered, putting the Partagás Culebra in his own mouth, "then smoke one of these. They're so mild even women like them . . ."

Firefly grabbed hold of the Havana with his two small moist hands; the silky texture and the warmth of the leaves surprised him. He was about to bring the cigar to his lips when the first ash burned his fingers. He blew on them, his eyes full of tears.

"I don't know how to smoke or how to whistle," he heard himself say. "No one ever taught me."

"Look," the scaly one replied, shaking with laughter, "nothing's easier." And he rubbed his hands together like a mason about to build a wall. "Haven't you ever seen a bat smoke?" *

He surged forward, and using thumb and forefinger like a pincer he held the boy's nose. Then he stuffed the cigar in his mouth. The little firefly began to choke.

Isidro was breaking up the bread crumbs left on the tablecloth and devouring them compulsively. He tried to make the doughy ones into figurines, but they all came out grotesque, like ugly big-nosed priests.

The poor buzzing insect managed to breathe in the smoke and cough it out. He clenched his belly, bent toward the floor, tried to throw up. But he could not. His red-rimmed eyes spun out of their orbits.

"Again, dammit!" was the executioner's only response. "Again! Let's see if you can learn!"

Firefly sucked in air. He thought about his sister. He looked around for help.

That was when Isidro, without a word, and with that instanta-

* So, the prediction returns.

neous energy only hatred can produce (had it germinated slowly between them like a miasma, an emanation of deep-seated rivalry or reciprocal envy?), knocked Gator aside with a sharp slap to the face.

The reptile teetered. He grabbed onto a chair. He straightened as if preparing to return the affront. Indignation made his eyes glassy. He looked at the kitchen knife. His right hand trembled for a moment . . . Then he turned toward the door, stepped determinedly through it, and slammed it shut behind him.

Without a glance at Firefly, without any gesture of reproval or satisfaction, and in no hurry, Isidro followed him.

The melon-head was left alone in the cubicle. A sick silence again took hold of everything, an exasperating calm, like after a curse. Or the filth of sex.

Firefly then contemplated the city from another window.

The sky was leprous. Humidity and heat, like acid, had corroded the soaring façades piled upon one another; purple peelings, like scabs or oozing cankers, curled from broken lintels, triangular porticos, and cracked volutes. On the sagging roofs nested seabirds, speckled lizards with spiny tails, raucous macaws, and mesmerized cats, indifferent to the hordes of rodents.

Making his way down the winding cobblestone alleys, amid

the cries of washerwomen and the scurrying of pickpockets and children, was an emaciated blond teenager, long-haired, barefoot, and bearded, wearing a violet-and-gold cape and hauling a wooden cross. With his right hand he held up a sign: crude red letters announced the apocalypse and called on the pope to reveal the prophecies of Fatima.

Heading in the other direction, unperturbed by the prediction, was a stout black man, his muscled chest shining with sweat, as if swathed in dusky silk, under the weight of the casket on his back.

The geometries of windows, semicircular arches held by slight copper frames, stood out in the fractured walls above doorways splayed permanently open. Scarlet, lime-green, mustard, and amethyst windowpanes projected daubs of color onto the tiled floors of darkened rooms, deforming their polished checker-boards of floral motifs and sweeping still lifes.

On one façade, above a trim of broken tiles and alongside a stucco niche containing a hairless and bloodied Christ with slanty eyes – a relic of Macao – a few tarnished gold letters remained.

Clothes floated on lines; flapping in the hot wind that presaged a storm were mended handkerchiefs, yellowing lace bedcovers, silver dresses, dazzling rags fit for welcoming an orisha's descent or for leading a sumptuous procession.

From afar came the sounds of raucous jingle bells, off-key

horns, and damp maracas from some fiesta; a strong aroma wafted in: grated coconut with butterscotch.

Downstairs, Firefly thought he heard something like the stumbling of a drunk. Then the big bolt opening. And the slamming of the door.

The wind blew hard. The rain had begun.

He understood then that *he was expecting someone, but was convinced that no one was going to come.*

Firefly out cold

He decided to escape. That morning he took a long look at himself in the mirror, deep into his own eyes. He ran his index finger along the fuzzy shadow above his lips. By now, his bamboo-flute tones were breaking into sudden bass notes that belonged to a voice nothing like his own: that of the someone else he would later become, but who was already keeping watch over him like a resourceful double from the vantage of his future, where all things appear ideal, incorruptible, until the present devours them.

He could make no sense of the reality around him. Such murkiness was lethal. The intrigue of the inexplicable visits, but one example of the pervasive darkness, threatened him like a daily warning blown his way by the Toothless One.

Suddenly one afternoon, like just before an earthquake, everything fell silent. The sky turned into a gray metal plate, insufferably heavy, that seemed to keep watch, mirrorlike.

The goldfish, as if struck by an electric current, jumped in unison out of the pond and did full somersaults on the cement floor up to the foot of the ceiba tree. As fast as he could, Firefly collected them and tossed them, still covered in dirt, back into the water. Though slowly, some of them began to swim again, seeming half asleep; others floated belly-up, shaken by brief spasms. Firefly scolded them, threatening famine, nets, feral cats, and he pushed them about with his cupped hands.

It was useless.

They lay at the edge, motionless except for a slight bobbing on the puny green-specked waves, lockjawed.

Firefly picked them up again, this time frantically. He dropped them into the deep holes where the lizards nest, down among the big strong roots of the ceiba.

The iron knocker on the main door rang out.

Munificence was waiting in the first-floor pantry with a tray of meringues, still warm, that she herself had painstakingly whipped and baked all morning long and whose whitish and satiny-wet appearance made them look more like the spiral excrement of a brooding hen than the refined output of a swanky patisserie.

She left the tray on a small round table and went to open the door.

It was two witches.

Each was enveloped in wrinkled, austere, uniform black, to which they had added black-and-white checkered headscarves whose ends draped like flexible chessboards around their necks and down their backs.

Crowning this cloak of armor was the unequivocal emblem of iniquity: mirrored sunglasses, which in place of the observing gaze return the intrigued spectator's own questioning image, miniaturized to reflect the true dimensions of his self-importance, just to bring him down a peg.

The two mourners, however, were quite distinct: complementary inverse omens of danger. Or better yet: snakes, which though already sated, suck on each other, perhaps to replenish their poisons. The one who entered first was stout and striking; despite her somber attire, around her hips garlands of lusty fat stood out, and jutting from under her kerchief were three decreasing rows of plump double chins. The other, on the contrary, was a long tall drink of water, her headscarf held in place by an intricate onyx brooch in the shape of two leaves of holly, which clawed at the fabric like a crab. As for her shoes, it looked like a frightened lizard had wrapped itself around her feet.

They mounted the stairs at full tilt without tripping or taking in the mess on the first floor, as if they already knew the ins and outs of the place. Munificence led the way, plate of meringues in hand, making Versailles-esque gestures and flustered excuses about the perpetual disorder that reigns among men of the law.

But there was something else: the Venetian tower that had always crowned her head like an albino battlement held erect by hair spray . . . was gone.

Supposedly enthralled by the latest fashion, Munificence had turned up at the barbershop pleading for the utter annihilation of that extravagant edifice. That was her way, she clarified exhilarated, of celebrating.

The haircut came out, Firefly noted, patchy, jagged, and bristly. Something did remain of those golden strands. But now they stood on end atop a bluish cranium, close-cropped around the sides. A veritable buzz cut, poor woman.

So the three of them went on up, in single file, heads down and in a hurry, united it seemed by the same resolve or at least wrapped in the same silence.

They entered one of the notaries' cubicles as if something inside were urging them on. The two desks were covered with unstable pyramids of dusty papers that seemed to have lain there for an eternity.

"Sit down a moment," Munificence begged, and after a pause,

"Knowing all too well that alcohol does not go with such matters, I've prepared some ice-cold lemonade. I'm going to the charity house to get it. But let me make it clear from the outset that I have not really explained to her what this is about, though being such a bright girl for her age she knows that to be a woman you have to suffer through many things like this. Even worse."

In a little while her footsteps could be heard returning. She carried a silver tray bearing a full pitcher with tinkling ice cubes surrounded by little gold-filigreed glasses. Ada walked before her, dressed all in white. Her socks came up to her knees and her shining red hair, plaited into a French braid, was held in place at the nape of her neck by two ivory pins.

When they entered the office they left an aroma of bitter lime, hair spray, and camphor in the stale air of the corridor.

"Ada," the stout one sprung on her once she had her face-to-face, "you are the oldest of the group. Your breasts are already showing."

And she brushed her graceful, pallid right hand against them like an emeritus emcee, deadpan.

"What we are going to do to you," skin-and-bones chimed in, her tinny voice interrupted by a nervous hiccup, "might nowadays seem abusive . . ." She took in air. Her bronchial tubes whistled like moist bellows.

"But once you are a full-grown woman," clarified her expansive accessory, "you will thank us with all your heart." She let out a sigh. "Come sit on this stool," she added sweetly.

"Here it is," was all Munificence managed to articulate. She drew from between her breasts an angular vial like a polyhedronic crystal of rainbow quartz that fit nicely the curve of her palm.

Ada began to sob. From a wide square pocket in the starched apron tied around her, like a kangaroo's pouch, she pulled an immaculate lace handkerchief, which she handed immediately to Munificence.

The newly shorn woman moistened it carefully by turning over the vial, which she held tight in the hollow of her left hand. An aroma of pounded leaves inundated the cubicle. The transparent and viscous concoction, with a slight green tint like snake's saliva or the sweat of a diseased orchid, left sticky stains on the fabric.

The gaunt one undid the brooch holding her headscarf, drew a shiny black thread, like the kind used for sutures, from between her breasts, and with it threaded the needle that, in place of a simple pin, had held the clasp in place.

"After this, I'm absolutely certain," murmured her heavy and haggard partner, "if for your fifteenth birthday you get the urge to put on – and she yanked the brooch from the skeletal hand, squinted her myopic turquoise eyes, and without further preamble drove the needle into the lobe of the redhead's right ear – the finest hoop earrings, you'll be able to do it," she concluded.

Ada's scream was an animal's pierced by an arrow tipped with curare, an unbearable howl.

She tried to break free while the obese woman knotted the black thread in her earlobe. Munificence pinned her arms, immobilizing her in the chair; the skinny one's wiry olive-skinned hands covered her mouth to stifle her shrieks.

"Think of the earrings, the earrings," the perforator repeated, her mouth very close by the left ear she was about to stick with the needle. Ada struggled in the claws of her executioners, a trapped prey.

Along with her tears fell minuscule drops of blood on the greenish leather desktop, on the empty silver tray, and on the piles of thick file folders softened by the heat and the humidity.

Munificence staunched the wound with the lace handkerchief, now a blood-soaked rag on which she kept smearing goop from the bottle.

They noted – winking at one another, if discreetly, fearfully – that the victim was growing pale; she rested her drooping head on the back of the easy chair; her eyes kept closing. A purplish stain like a sick jellyfish spread across her eyelids. She was sweating. Her lips were white.

"Hang on," Munificence ordered the busy perpetrators. She watched Ada uneasily and with pity, perhaps even an unexpected love. "Let's wait until she recovers before we continue. A bit of lemonade, with lots of sugar."

But she would not drink.

Then they rubbed her face with a slice of lime. Munificence began to speak to her quietly, to awaken her: "Ada, Ada, the worst is over. We'll do the rest another day. Think of the earrings."

The scarecrow restrung the clasp's needle to achieve some symmetry.

Fatso slipped pieces of ice between the girl's lips.

The afternoon heat had become suffocating and dense. A salty breeze wafted in. A bolt of lightning streaked the sky.

Ada opened her eyes.

They were about to carry on when suddenly they heard something bulky collapse on the first floor like a landslide. Then silence.

Munificence went slowly, noiselessly to the door. She yanked it open and went out fuming.

Down the stairs she went, stamping furiously on each step. When she reached the lower floor she could contain herself no longer. "As if I hadn't had enough!" she shrieked. "As if I hadn't had enough! Now Firefly's out cold!"

"*Lethargy cubensis*," diagnosed the intern, excessively learned like all apprentices, "a typical case."

He glanced out of the corner of his eye at the spot where his idle supervisor stood beside a Victrola, listening attentively to a scratchy record and swinging a stethoscope in his hand.

Firefly lay on a low cot between two cabinets of surgical instruments, duly burnished and classified, displayed on glass shelves. The sharp edges of the aluminum bistouries and pincers sparkled in the stale and morbid air of that municipal clinic located next door to the charity house, a refuge of the penniless and the thunderstruck, where lowly students aided renowned physicians in the most trivial or unpleasant sanitary tasks.

When anyone ran down the hall or strode by like a boxer or a boss, the instruments of incision vibrated with a tiny tinkling.

Anatomy charts and silent-film posters covered the walls. Besides the nasal sound of the record player, there was rumbling from a water pump, chirping from a few birds, and, closer by, the groans of a patient.

Munificence, seated on a wire stool and reading an old copy of *Hola*, awaited the intern's verdict.

Firefly swiveled his right hand back and forth, signaling from his cot, "I'm not great."

"We're going to do a blood test," the assistant clarified, addressing Munificence. He overarticulated the words, the way one shouts to someone far away or speaks to the deaf.

Firefly felt like he was naked and alone in a marble room, covered with an ice-cold sheet. From head to foot.

The intern opened up the cabinet and pulled out a syringe and a tourniquet. He raised the syringe in the air and held it to the light, slowly pushing and pulling the plunger to see if it was working. He went over to Firefly, who watched him, sweaty and frozen.

He wore a white cap secured at the forehead with an elastic band, and a doctor's coat, open and starched. Below that, a shirt and a silk tie with painted dragonflies and big golden blooms held in place by a clip. Baggy pants, tied at the waist and ankles with white cords.

"Make a fist, real tight." He tied the tourniquet around Firefly's upper arm. "Think of something else."

Firefly heard a loud buzzing in his ears.

Then the voice of his sister. But he could not tell what she was saying.

Nor what happened after that.

POEM FROM PLAZA DEL VAPOR

He spent his final charity-house days absorbed in his pious part as the gofer, the errand boy on permanent probation, the flunky bargaining for brownie points for an improbable posterity. He gave up his nocturnal snooping, slept naked and forsaken, his feet propped up on the varnished mahogany volute of the reca-mier, which could no longer contain both him and the disarray of disheveled dockets. Now he dreamed and it was always the same: He was saying goodbye to his mother in a place divided by walls made of thick fractured glass; he reproached her for allow-ing him to leave (as if something that happened much later were occurring at that very moment), for not insisting he stay on at home. He felt the warm maternal skin of her arms and face so singularly close that he was convinced they were real. When they were about to part, he would wake up in tears.

One day his feet nudged a few of the documents as he awoke, and he realized he could read the lawyers' letterheads and even their signatures. No one had taught him. Unless you could call it teaching when the big-shot lawyers, laughing and tugging on his earlobe, would point at a letterhead and shout out syllable by syllable the surname printed there. The day he first arrived on the arm of the black Santeria priestess, Munificence showed him Christ on an alphabet card all dog-eared and yellowed.

"The rest is too hard for you," she said and, as if she wanted to make sure no one could reach it, she stuck the abecedary between the leaves of the acanthus molding on a false column, a fleetingly popular stucco ornamentation in what once had been the impeccable front room of the lower floor. "I'll teach you," she added peevishly, "one letter a day."

But he never got any follow-up ABC's, nor did he manage to decipher the intricate ink symbols on his own after he managed, high on a folding stepladder, to steal the dusty rolled-up card from amid the Corinthian foliage.

With the same security – that irretrievable feeling which emanates from innocence and which all knowledge corrupts – with which he had once pronounced "decimeter, centimeter" perfectly without knowing its meaning, like a spell against fear, he now took hold of a quill pen lying on the desk next to the recamier.

He moistened the moldy tip in the depths of an inkpot; all that remained was a thick, dirty, black paste, like sediment from medicine or extract from poison. On a vellum paper envelope he sketched several laconic and authoritative squiggles without a clue as to their meaning: something, no doubt, that he had better remember.

He spent that day imagining inscriptions, which he visualized distinctly in his mind's eye on a red background, embellished with arabesques and gold filigree.

From the drawer of a mortgage broker he stole a notebook with big cottony pages, wide margins, and horizontal turquoise lines; from the satchel where a tax official hid his clutter, he snitched a pencil. He slipped them both carefully into the front pocket of his trousers. He felt the binding of the notebook rubbing against his sex, the iridescent seam like a soft piece of mother-of-pearl caressing him throughout the day, while he, docile lackey, hurried down the long corridors of the office building.

Afternoon again came to an end in Plaza del Vapor. They had not yet closed the slaughterhouses, the rag dealers, the cinnamon shops. Glowing inside the darkened stores, as if touched by the last rays of sunset, were the silver threads of Indian fabric, the purple of dyes, the misshapen spice jars that still conserved their fleur-de-lis insignia, old colonial coats of arms, lacquered seals from provincial apothecaries, or the still-legible emblem of the Compañía de Indias. Moneylenders packed away their etched-glass lamps and their strongboxes inlayed with sandalwood, ebony, and jacaranda; a hand with rings over black-gloved fingers unpinned from the edge of a shelf a square of black velvet displaying large irregular coins whose royal profiles were cracked, and another featuring little cellophane envelopes overflowing with vibrantly colored triangular stamps from countries that had disappeared or never existed.

A squalid apprentice dressed in white, stinking of soy sauce and shellac (his limp and shiny black hair hung down his back) unhooked from an oxblood-red wall a sign that announced in impulsive angry letters, like ideograms, a brief, amenable Cantonese menu. At least that is what Firefly managed, more than read, to guess. Or make up.

He took an alley that dropped sharply to the docks, as did the storm sewer that ran down its center, where the Indian women, before heading off to the tenements where they crowded in for the night, washed up their offspring, watered the tree rodents they kept in cages, and spread on the cobblestones the rags they had pounded with their fists and then wrapped, still moist, in the filthy rucksacks they carried on their backs.

The fork to the right was less inviting: ruins of those big neo-classical homes with Corinthian columns, frontispieces, and fleur-de-lis heraldry that sugar magnates coveted back in the early republican era, today the domain of fiery red brambles, liz-ard colonies, single-minded mice, and two tramps. Beggars were simultaneously reproach and entertainment in the city's older neighborhoods, which accepted them as eccentric residues of the twisted fauna engendered by the Machado dictatorship, when a person's daily ration was a "blond with green eyes" – a plate of rough flour with two slices of avocado.

The grand seigneur of that couple was the Gentleman from Paris, who dressed in a black velvet cape in the suffocating heat of the island summer, his chest armored with ancient newspa-pers and magazines, and who spouted an ardent prosopopoeia featuring backwards tropes worthy of Lezama or of Chicharito and Sopeira, which he proffered in impeccable Castilian diction.

His unhinged partner was the Marchioness, a splotchy-skinned, gray-haired black woman with an easy stride and Versailles-esque manners, the play protégé of witty dissolute ladies and even of real marchionesses (to the degree the woody worm-eaten branches of insular heraldry allowed), who dressed her in outlandish attire left over from presidential balls or some bash at the Tropicana where the gowns had been ordered from the finest of Erté's disciples.

At the far end of that dump for architectonic and human ruins rose a solitary and dilapidated tower, the incongruent remains of a fortress that turned out to be indefensible or had been simply abandoned by commanders who were insolvent or had been relieved in mid-construction, to which several flamboyant volutes had given a vague Antillean Gothic look. No one went near it, nor did anyone even mention it (and when they did it was with their fingers making the cross), to the point that it was presumed haunted and cursed.

He spotted the girls right away, at the end of the alleyway. There were two.

They were seated on folding chairs on the sidewalk, but backwards with the chair backs between their open legs. Their brocade outfits dragged on the ground; they wore pierced hoop earrings that reached their shoulders and tortoiseshell hairpins perched on the crowns of their heads. The tight black spirals of their kiss-curls outlined a lattice of rigid volutes on their foreheads and temples. The edges of their purple lips were underscored with a line of black. Their eyelids were two half-moons of trembling aluminum that flashed up and down like the fins of frightened fish.

A sour stench of sweat, beer, or rancid semen emanated from the interior of the sleazy dive behind them, along with a bluish blinking from the jukebox, drunken laughter and shouts, and a roll of raucous castanets.

"Are you ready to try it out?" one of the sparkling hussies murmured at once, fluttering her eyes for effect and pointing to his crotch.

"Do you know what it's for?" added the other. And she let out a stentorian cackle, stamping her heel on the ground and spreading her legs even farther apart. From the sidewalk she picked up a glass half full of a light green phosphorescent liquid, which she knocked back. She shook her head as if to pull herself together, snorted, and collected the tortoiseshell clasp, which had rolled to the curb. She shouted back into the bar, asking for more "fresh herb."

Her dancing partner was smoking very thin cigars, the ends of which she tapped, like a woodpecker opening a hole in a tree, against an oversized cigarette case encrusted with shining costume jewels in the shape of a hammer and sickle.

"A present," she explained to Firefly without him asking a

thing, "from the captain of a Russian ship that broke down at the refineries in the port and now – nothing lasts forever – on his way back to Kiev." She sighed. "*Katalavenis?*" she added, chuckling, and she lit another Partagás Culebrita.

From the square came the screech of a streetcar, and from a radio nearby the first chords of a tune.

The voices and guitars hung suspended for a moment in the air, along with a whiff of hot coffee, before being lost amid the bells of women selling java, the cries of vendors, and the blaring of car horns:

> *You like Carola, yes you really do,*
> *Here's a song from the hills*
> *To dance when it's just you two*
> *Feeling every thrill . . .*

"Go on in," the gaudy smoker practically scolded, once she had settled down. "No charge for the first time. And above all," she added, pointing to her bewildered double with a grimace of repulsion, "don't go with this strumpet. She'll do it all hurry-scurry and wrong. 'Cause that's what she is: *a fiendish she-devil.*"

The room was vaster than could be imagined from the street.

A life-size Saint Barbara encased in glass with her feudal battlements and her tin sword reigned in a back-wall niche next to a wrought-iron window. Beyond those black arabesques lay a yard filled with pots of flowering geraniums, a stone staircase, and an artesian well with a bucket and pulley.

A very thin strip of palpitating red neon outlined the niche's upper arch and extended in a straight line, interrupted in two tiny spots by electric wires, along a shelf filled with bottles, casting on the mauve wallpaper an orange glow in the shape of an awning that faded progressively as it reached up toward the rosette on the ceiling. Flies were drawn to that incandescent thread to immolate themselves with a zap of electrocuted elytra.

The scarlet mantle of the virgin saint threw a shadow on a stemmed bowl of ripe apples continually replenished at her feet.

Venturing in from the yard, up to the wrought-iron window, and then into the room itself in small wary leaps, looking all ways at once, a tomeguin finch came to peck at the fruit.

The stone staircase led from the purple yard up to the whores' bawdy hideaway.

As Firefly approached the first steps, an overpowering feeling of humiliation gripped him.

Andalusians were supposed to be lookers, lovely and clean,

glowing, funny and fat-cheeked, but when he climbed the stone staircase and entered their garret crammed with shelving, Firefly saw these two were pasty and out of shape, caked with gaudy make-up and stinking of patchouli. And what could be said of the faux-Spanish decor? Sets of three- or four-board white shelves covered every wall, the end pieces drilled full of holes like delicate Mozarabic lace and each shelf chockablock with large costumed dolls in iconic flamenco postures that sent the flounces and pet-ticoats of their teeming trains swirling down in a froth of vivid glowing colors.

Their little removable porcelain arms were bent backwards, revealing blackened rusty joints at the elbows and wrists; their fingers were set in various gestures; their dainty faces, incredibly white masks with long shining curled eyelashes and perfectly symmetrical arched eyebrows, seemed to be watching from the depths of their big opalescent glass eyes. They winked, astonished or flirtatious, whenever the chubby girls rocked them in their cushiony arms. Their cute little mouths were minuscule crimson hearts. Reigning over them, upright and flexible as a bulrush, was a string-puppet toreador.

"It's so hot!" one of the plump girls exclaimed as she let loose her hair. She placed the mother-of-pearl clasp on one of the shelves, at the foot of a frolicking chanteuse.

She shook her head vigorously, as if she had just emerged from a dip in the river.

The liberated locks opened into a rigid fan, like the marble curls of a Greek athlete, old-fashioned and taut.

"Feels like we're going to suffocate," the other added, pulling her dress over her head in one fell swoop.

She rolled it up and threw it furiously to the floor, like a rag.

All that was left were high-heels and a shining whalebone corset whose struts shaped and held her, a Venus about to burst from abundance or excessive bliss.

The three of them looked at one another against the multicolored cascade tumbling from the shelves, all red polka dots, stiff flounces, bows, and ruffles. One, corseted and majestic like a saint in a rural procession; Firefly, in his little white outfit and his narrow leather tie, a Texan at a fair; the other, crowned and circumspect, displaying her double chin like a turtledove at its most lyrical. While the latter stroked the cheeks of the novice with the tips of her purple nails, she tendered monosyllabic gurgles of voluptuousness in a husky, diabolical basso profundo.

"Well, what do we do now?" asked the trembling cowboy swinging his head from side to side to contemplate one after the other his good-natured corruptors.

"Now?" they asked back in unison, and they glanced at each

other in astonishment and unleashed the hoarse gravelly cackle of hardened smokers or fools at the end of a zarzuela. "Sandwich!" they decided concisely.

Firefly gaped at them perplexed, doing his best to untangle the libidinal riddle, but the arduous mental effort was short-lived: one of the brutes, making use of all the potent and wide-ranging strength in the giant pistons of her arms, pushed him down onto the cot.

He fell face-first on the old quilt, whose aroma he recognized straightaway, immobilized as he was by his abuser's brawny mitts: it smelled of old witch's fingers, the way Munificence's did when she got mad and started smacking her pupils and her knuckles would turn red and hot. Could that pitiless plotter be the mother of these pseudo-Sevillians? And if that were the case, why were they not living at her place, capable as they seemed, sewing and singing, instead of pursuing such a strange line of work?

Facedown on the stinking coverlet, sniffing the threads, gnawed at by the impatience and fear that overtook his body like lashings of hail, Firefly awaited the surprise of sex.

He did not have to wait long.

While one of the deflowerers held him down with her big hand, the other, at once conscientious and distant, efficient as a hired mourner at a moneyed wake, stuck her fingers in his pants at the waist without undoing the button or the belt. That soft flat hand, warm, shaken slightly by brief tremors, as if the chubby girl's breathing or talk were rippling through her entire body, was like the silk of the recamier: smooth, ready for a rub, both comfy and tense against his sex, alongside the notebook and pencil still in his pocket.

The other hand, the ham that held him to the bed, open against his back and now lower down, sheltered above the curve of his ass as if its volume coincided precisely with that hollow, began to move lazily up and down like it was squeezing a Turkish pillow or gesturing, "Slow down, slow down."

Firefly closed his eyes, took a deep breath like the prelude to a sigh, recalled what he had felt when the porcelain chamber pot slid down the cistern with him hanging on to the handles, besieged by his aunts' chortles in the purple shade of the cockatoo-filled royal poinciana, until the basin smashed against the floor. He felt it again now: a cramp making its way up through his tummy.

It was nighttime. He was at the beach. The water was oily, warm, and black; sea wasps swam about. Flying fish sailed like daggers from one wave to the next. He let himself drift, facedown in the water. A cool breeze caressed his back. From the shore, his sister called to him, "Firefly! Firefly!" But he paid no heed. The voice was unreal, too far off, or maybe imitated by somebody else. Nothing mattered more than this sense of abandon, this languorous release to the waves.

Now, the upper hand descended as well, sliding under his belt, caressing his ass. He felt the outsized fingers resting on his skin, three on one of his cheeks, two on the other. Then, the longest fell carelessly into the crack. Now he felt two fingers on one side and two on the other, the long one going a bit deeper with each oscillation, rubbing the cleft as if by accident. Suddenly, the manipulator flipped him over so he was faceup, panting; her hand slipped in his fly, and then her warm, moist tongue.

He was in a barbershop full of cracked mirrors and jars topped with long rubber tubes and pestles for pulverizing alcohol and amber. It smelled of Arabic gum, rubbing oil, old men. It might have been his first visit to the barber.

"Have you ever seen it?" one of the mulatto barbers asked jokingly while peeking at Firefly out of the corner of his eye. He was taking care of an old gray-haired guy in the next seat who had a toothpick between his lips and a shirt with mother-of-pearl buttons open to his navel.

"What?" answered his big-bellied partner, feigning interest while he stirred a pot of foam and brushed light touches of soap on his customer's throat.

"The crack," the brown-skinned man clarified in a suppressed whisper, faking unease, as if this were the first time they had ever exchanged this tomfoolery.

"What crack?"

"Come on, in your behind."

"No, never."

"Oh . . ."

"So, how do you do it?"

Here the lewd tutor glanced again at Firefly, perhaps to indicate that the perverse instructions were meant for him.

"You put a mirror on the floor . . ."

"And then?" Big-belly had stopped shaving and was listening, his razor motionless against his customer's throat, surprised, exuding innocence, as if this were his first exposure to the perplexing procedure.

"Well, then," continued the impudent mulatto, "you squat on it."

Firefly had felt a weight on his chest. Now, while the plump girl's finger ran around the edge, poked about, now to slip in, now to touch the inside, and now that the oscillation, the soft undulation emanated from that finger, he felt the same pressure again, as if all the bifurcations of the bronchial tree were swollen shut and the air was stuck at the crossroads, incapable of choosing a path, until it lost its usual clarity, became charred and deadly.

While he shuddered, sweated, believed he was going to lose all his blood through his sex, while everything spilled out into the indolent hand, the two girls chatted happily, untouched by the novice's astonishment, pleasure, anguish. The whores challenged each other with demented riddles, wild and repetitive like scratched phonograph records.

"I want something but I don't know what it is."
"I know. Let me tell you. Is it something sweet?"
"Yes . . ."
"Cold?"
"Yes . . ."
"White?"
"Yes . . ."
"With rum?"
"Yes."
"*Crème de vie!*"

When he came back downstairs, he noticed the jukebox in the dance hall was playing. Dull goofy music flowed from the machine. Handclaps and castanets. Dancing in front of it, illuminated by the greenish glow from the buttons, was a very thin child dressed only in a white linen cloth tied around his waist. When he raised his hands to snap his fingers, all his ribs showed. He followed the rhythm but was distracted, absent, staring into space, as if his true self were somewhere else and he was only repeating to exhaustion the steps from a lesson. His skin was brown and dry. His incredibly long hair swung when he turned his head, or when he tilted forward and then unexpectedly to the side or back. With his narrow white feet he kept time on the cool tiles.

Firefly remained silent, riveted.

He thought hard about Ada.

And he cried.

The urge to laugh

By the time he left, everything had changed. It could have been a different day.

The jukebox was quiet. The little Gypsy, now completely naked, was asleep on his white cloth spread on the cool of the cement floor in one corner of the room. It looked like he was listening to a seashell.

The street was silent and deserted. Either it was already getting light or the sky was strangely heavy and white. The paving stones glistened as if it had rained.

A greenish smoke from hookahs clogged with red crud wafted through the window grates and from under the doors of the Chinese stores. A passerby could hear the raspy sound of frail bodies moving on reed mats.

Back to the storm sewer marched the Indian women. Slowly, in single file, bent under their rucksacks or under layers of white gladiolas, which they carried from the edge of the city to sell in markets before the sun wilted the blooms.

The gulls that nested amid the broken panes of clerestories in colonial palaces, or in abandoned pigeon coops on the roofs of the mansions of exiles, returned to the masts and to the first garbage offered by early-rising sailors, on-board scullions.

From behind a weathered door, which looked to be on its last legs, made of darker, denser wood than most, came the sound of canticles.

Firefly figured a believer was tuned in to the Vatican radio station, attending from afar, as often happened, the canonization of some pious islander or the promulgation of an incendiary encyclical on the nascent, forbidden church of liberation.

Following an old habit, almost by reflex, he pressed his ear to the wood above the cast-bronze knocker (a lion's head with a ring in its nose, its mane combed and even), whose chill he felt against his cheek.

The door swung open on a dark corridor.

Cautiously, Firefly made his way in. The corridor led to a cloister with rudimentary but ornate columns on which small tiles, bits of coral, coins, fishing lures, and pieces of colored glass all sparkled in the rising sun like tiny golden mirrors.

The capitals of the columns featured shaggy demons vomiting

flames, or angelic priests whose smiles the mildew had transformed into sickening grimaces.

A sunburned lawn that looked to be made of spiky metal wires instead of grass covered the little garden, interrupted by bald spots of clumpy, rusty, red dirt.

From the fountain in the middle (the same decorative trinkets as on the columns depicted gorgonian faces, but they were incomplete, one-eyed, worn away) rose, intermittently, a feeble, foolish spurt of water.

They filled a chapel painted blue with gold stars, on the far side of the garden, across from the doorway where Firefly had come in. They were dressed in rough white robes, the hoods folded back, their faces olive-skinned and severe.

Moving slowly, deliberately, they broke bread on a bare altar, the only ornamentation a simple wooden cross.

Wrapped in her purple mantle, a slant-eyed virgin twisted in on herself like a fiery S looked down from a wooden ledge; gold outlined the concentric folds of the fabric at her knees. The lateral predellas were occupied by the donors, counts from Jaruco, kneeling in prayer.

Suddenly he was shaken by an absurd hunch, the very possibility of which was enough to disconcert him: Could this be the charity-house chapel that was always closed up, except when a young priest aired it out between Easter and Saint John's Day, and he had arrived by another entrance? *

He understood then, in a way as inescapable and true as death, that he lacked something inherent to life, something so obvious that others did not even know they had it: a sense of direction.

At a fork in the road he had no idea what to do, just as he had no idea what to do when faced with the ritual – no doubt second nature to others – of sex.

He sensed in an opaque way, as if he had received an unspoken but fatal warning, that he would always be lost, disoriented, lacking an interior compass, as if the entire Earth were a laborious labyrinth or a perverse mirage of movable walls someone had contrived just to get him lost, to bring him down.

A grizzled and toothless old woman in rags distributed with careful disequilibrium, like she had been dressed to play a lep-

* Have you ever heard of bibliomancy? It's a form of divination that one can turn to only a few times in life if it is to "work," and that consists of opening the Bible at random and pointing to a line without looking at the page.

I have done it twice in my lifetime, at moments of great need. The first came up Matthew 2:12 (The Flight into Egypt): "And being warned of God in a dream that they should not return to Herod, they departed into their own country another way."

This is a call to seers: What was Saint Matthew trying to tell me?

[118]

rous beggar in a sacramental rite, came noiselessly toward him. Hanging by its feet from her right hand was a dead canary, which she set down delicately, perhaps afraid she might harm it, next to a little basket.

"Madam," Firefly addressed her, his voice quavering, fearing maybe he might spoil the offering of the bird.

"What?" the mendicant in disguise answered grudgingly, smoothing her matted yellowish-white mane and breathing deeply, as if offended by an unpardonably foul remark or a flouting of the most common courtesy.

"What chapel is this?" Firefly chanced, like someone who dares to utter a blasphemy or a provocation.

"The chapel of the Virgin, can't you see?"

"But . . ."

"But what?"

"Those monks . . ."

"They're singing, can't you see?" and she turned her back, annoyed by what she considered morbid ridicule or pretend curiosity.

Then he was forced to realize further, from this very evidence, that he would never have anyone to orient him, that for others his deficiency was like a vice, deliberate and embraced with malicious delight, that ought to be outlawed and exterminated.

He felt blindfolded and alone at the center of a grotesque, cackling circle spinning around him. People delighted in his being lost, the way his aunts had delighted at his defecation.

His body, the laws of his body, gave people the urge to laugh.

The canticles faded away.

But the dull hum of the vowels from the invocation remained hanging in the air like a vocal residue: reversed and inaudible, yet precise.

And now, after a pause in which they were still and silent, the monks, like brothers after a separation, like blood relatives after a long absence, hugged and kissed one another, celebrating a ritual reunion, a holy day, or a resurrection.

Visible through the windows, and at the same time reflected in them, were the monks' scrawny bodies: white robes, knotted ropes, crude wooden crosses. The starry indigo sky of the chapel met the reflection of the lawn's burned greenery and the precarious squirt of water. A very fine line, broken and red, marked the border between them.

Superimposed on those reflections, Firefly now saw senseless images whipping by, the way it is supposed to happen seconds before death. Swollen, splintered, warped, colors and shapes morphing, one image becoming another, turning monstrous, distorted, helix-like, gilded: in the foreground, occupying the entire windowpane, a gloved hand with ringed fingers spread wide pulling down the coins . . . in the background, fragile and fleeting minutiae, mosaics viewed underwater, dots and streaks (the hookers' rigid, black-dyed kiss-curls) . . . the notary's drawer that opened with a yank . . . a gleaming light swinging and spinning before his eyes (the pendulum) . . . Ada's perfume . . . a target . . . the wrinkled face of an old woman like doodles in beeswax . . . the taste of *crème de vie* . . . a hand on his sex, large and pink like gum . . . the chamber pot sliding down the cistern . . .

"What they call writing," he then said to himself, "must be just that: to be able to make some order out of things and their reflections."

One by one, the monks genuflected before the altar, crossed themselves, and began to leave.

"If I could write," he continued, "I could make things appear and disappear as they really are instead of the jumbled way they look in the window, all mixed up with their reflections."

The chapel was empty. Still he dared not step in. An intensity, an invisible texture in the air held him back. To enter would be to violate the memory the room held of the silence and, earlier, of the meditations and voices.

He remembered that he still had the stolen notebook and

pencil in his pocket. He pulled them out and on the first page drew a few shapeless scribbles, grotesque ideograms, which he aligned vertically. Then he erased them and replaced them with others equally inept. God knows what they might be. But for him the meaning was utterly clear:

Poem
from
Plaza
del
Vapor

Disillusion

Fresh salt air, reeking of the sea. The purplish-blue shadows of things seemed to swirl around him, as if a crazed moon were spinning about the sky. Or maybe what had changed was his own body, inhabited now by somebody else.

Down the shining cobblestone street came a skeletal black calash driver with chiseled cheekbones, at this hour already dressed in his vest and bowler hat. He stepped lightly, almost weightlessly, practically floating over the paving stones. With his right arm he pushed a loose cartwheel; in his free hand he carried a whip. The wheel bounced on the stones, wobbled, continued downhill.

When the coachman passed Firefly, he gave him a surprised look, as if he recognized him and wondered what he was doing out there at that time of day.

Cautiously, at a distance, like an affectionate and obliging mother, someone was following the driver.

Firefly first recognized the starched white housedress, which ruffled open in the humid morning breeze like an immense day lily; then, shining just as white, the necklaces, small friendly seashells whose rattling he thought he could discern; and finally, the bright silk turban: the black Santeria priestess had found him again.

In her hands she carried a lantern, its light extinguished, its glass stained from smoke, as if she had been using it all night long on her travels.

"You are going to discover something beside the water," the mother of saints told him at once. Her voice was that of a woman who had just swallowed a sip of honey.

"How do you know?"

The priestess rattled her necklaces. "And what's more," she added smiling, "it'll happen soon. You'll never go back home after seeing what you are about to see."

She half turned on her heels, like someone finishing a dance or jubilant at having completed a mission. She raised her hand and called to the coachman. Firefly understood neither the name she called out nor the language she spoke.

They greeted each other with a salutation Firefly had never seen: mother's right shoulder touched the driver's left, then they repeated the same gesture in reverse.

They disappeared up a cobblestone alley between two pink churches. In the fragile light of dawn, the two figures against the sparkling bluish paving stones fresh with dew had the precision of a mirage: morning's white lingering note, ephemeral messengers who vanished before the sun could devour everything with its leprous cruelty.

The churches' symmetrical façades glowed like unfinished metal when the first orange rays of the sun touched the broken volutes and the gross adipose angels shaking maracas on either side of the doors and beside the crumbling triangle of lintels, where invading rats had found all the amenities of refuge.

Firefly took a few steps. The joins between the cobblestones wove an awkward tangle, a perspective drawing of short drab lines that stood out against the leaden gray of the rilievos and receded progressively toward the horizon between the two churches.

He was meditating on the priestess's words and on everything in his life that seemed confused, ominous, and impossible to decipher. His story was a frayed tapestry with no apparent pattern, seen in a dream.

He felt someone touch him on the shoulder.

Startled, he turned around. He had not heard anyone approach.

Next to him stood a strange being somewhere between senile childhood and long-lasting decrepitude, maybe a girl whose face was parchment-like from premature wrinkles, or perhaps an elderly woman whose skin was smeared with wax or powdered eggshell. She was tiny, fragile-looking; her body had either not yet reached maturity or was already desiccated, skin and bone, and had preserved at the end of her life, like an archaeological relic, some aspect of her youth. She was wearing a long, baggy dress made of shining silk, within which she seemed to float. She was barefoot. Her feet were bony and pointy, and against the paving stones they looked like two porgies. Her hair was straw-blond, maybe newborn fuzz or maybe gray, dyed with peroxide and saffron. A flimsy tiara made of hammered silver or tin held and adorned her lustrous scalp.

The lips of the apparition parted in a hint of a smile or a grimace. From the depths of her foggy pupils streaked with ash this emaciated being glanced his way. "Would you like me to show you something?" she accosted him without the least preamble. "Something you will never forget?"

"Who are you?" Firefly managed to mumble as he stepped

back, terrified by the possibly angelic, possibly demonic, certainly supernatural specter.

"You don't recognize me?" the horror responded with derision. Her voice was fluty and nasal; her phrases ended with a piercing rasp. "Take a good look because I haven't changed. Don't you remember the day Munificence on a whim kicked me out of the charity house? Ah, now you see who I am!" and her voice exploded in a gravelly chortle.

She raised her skirts and spun around, slender and supple.

Firefly (he always noticed the trifling and missed the essential) noted that she spun in the opposite direction to the priestess. The silk of her dress sparkled with a bluish glint in the square, like a standard in a procession.

"What are you doing here so early?" Firefly asked.

"I was at a masked ball at the Colonia Española, and I gave my tutors the slip so I could take a stroll on my own. Would you like me to show you something? A place like no other. If you come, you won't regret it."

She gave him a tremulous wink of her waxy eyelids that was meant to be mischievous. Then she touched his shoulder lightly in a gesture suggesting complicity, which to Firefly felt like the caress of a scorpion.

The skinny girl did not knock on the door; she shoved it open.

A descending spiral staircase came into view; it had no banister, nor did it appear to ever end. Down below reigned a greenish penumbra populated by indecipherable murmurs: black wings or poisonous elytra.

The descent seemed interminable.

Skin-and-bones went first, whirling frenetically and shouting gleeful encouragement, which her nasal twang and the metallic timbre of the echo transformed into incomprehensible whines.

The train of her dress, always just a few paces ahead of Firefly, slithered over the stone steps like a lizard, only to reappear a spiral farther down.

Someone was descending ahead of them. Firm, confident steps perfectly at home. Suddenly a skid, something scattering on the floor – papers, a document, sheets flying. Silence.

Down, down they went.

But they found nothing.

At the end of that around-and-around, they came upon another door, this one covered with cushiony cockroach-infested bottle-green padding. It had a window.

Vulgar and determined, the runt opened it with a resounding kick.

The room had a high vaulted ceiling and a circular floor with inlaid bronze lettering. At the apex of the cupola was a brilliant porphyry dove. More doves decorated the rest of the ceiling, progressively diminishing in size and intensity of color from the tops of the walls to the zenith, the highest ones reduced to faded freaks, formless dull amoebae.

Red-and-purple tapestries covered the walls.

In their dense weave, amid bits of thread coming loose at the edges, stains from the humidity, holes, and burn marks, were scenes Firefly could not comprehend: a chubby white blond woman, naked, her skin iridescent, was licking the hard orange bill of a gigantic duck with greasy blue feathers, standing tall and proud like a billy goat. Down the neck of the bird slid fresh raindrops or dew; in his eyes shone a spark of desire more human than animal.

Framing that twisted coupling were garlands of orchids and sprays of royal poinciana blossoms, among which weird rollicking hybrids performed acrobatic feats: pairings of dissimilar beasts, grotesque graftings that defied understanding and parodied reason.

Atop the pistils of an open flower, alighted a flying shrimp with bat's wings and a crown; between two leafless branches soared a mouse with fins, driven by a boat propeller.

In the tapestry's upper-right-hand corner, as if breaking free from the woof and weft, a hummingbird reigned in fixed flight.

Seated on the little wicker chairs found in rural or impoverished churches, sullen old men trembling with impatience waited in silence, several of them in *dril cien* suits and straw hats that they spun nervously in their laps when they were not crossing and uncrossing their legs.

Firefly remained motionless behind the door, which had swung shut, contemplating that viscous spectacle: The rectangular glass window deformed the faces, flattening cheekbones and noses, as if someone had taken sandpaper to them.

"About time, little madam, about time," exclaimed the most pallid and potted of the old crocks. "All the blessed night waiting for you. And now that you're here at last, you've come, if I understand correctly, empty-handed. Isn't that the case?"

A dry little cough made him shudder.

"Not at all, gentlemen, not at all," the scrawny girl answered, feigning offense. "Surprises await. But please, a little patience."

"Surprises? At this point?" replied the elderly man with a hint of incredulity. "So, where are they?"

"For the time being," the withered girl responded as she backed away, "keep your eyes on the waterfall, that always calms the nerves. And have some coffee with a nice glass of cold papaya wine."

She let out a cackle and stepped toward a folding screen set up on the other side of the room.

A large curved window of thick glass, like a jeweler's loupe, interrupted the succession of tapestries and their grim copulations, and distorted the view of what lay beyond: a Japanese garden, complete with squares of raked sand, bonsai trees, and a waterfall, the whole of it stretched like elastic at the edges, bulging in the center, and excessively illuminated by footlights of all colors.

Despite the glass window, the chatter in the room, and the cushiony covering on the door, Firefly could hear water splashing faintly.

Evaporation created a perpetual rainbow, smooth and motionless, above the polished rocks and the dwarf bushes that embraced the extremes of a little wooden bridge lacquered in red.

A sudden squeal of hinges suggested the inverted tower they were in had a hidden, surely minuscule, entry on the side opposite the spiral staircase.

There was silence.

Steps behind the folding screen. Firefly could make out a few voices in the distance, unrecognizable.

More silence.

In the room, someone getting up knocked over one of the little chairs, which smacked sharply against the floor like a whip or a slap.

Slow steps echoed under the vault.

In front of the suddenly animated audience (murmurs and exclamations were promptly repeated by the domed ceiling), right there, dressed in white, stood Ada.

The sight of her came and went instantaneously in Firefly's eyes, because all he could perceive was his heart exploding, something in his breast shattering into a thousand pieces.

"My god," was all he managed to think. "My body's so faulty and frail, how could I possibly endure such pain?"

He tried to breathe, but his chest was already a well filled with poison.

His bronchial tubes were made of glass and they wounded him as they splintered. He was freezing, he thought about his sister, he needed air. In trying to breathe, he emitted a high-pitched whistle tasting of rust and unbrushed teeth.

He was drenched in sweat. He smelled the foul odor of his own perspiration. His knees trembled.

That was when one of the venerable gentlemen, with an abrupt gesture as if making a superhuman effort to break a spell or a tableau vivant, stepped forward from the enraptured group and reached the place where the girl selected for the ritual, perhaps by now resigned to it, awaited.

With the tip of his index finger, carefully, as if he did not wish to offend her, almost with diffidence, he touched her on the forehead.

And he tasted a drop of her sweat.

Ada was pallid. An involuntary tremor seemed to take hold of her starting from her hands, a sudden iciness rising from her feet. Who knows why she sent her gaze upward; perhaps she did not want to face the men's eager eyes resting unctuously on her body, their moist maneuvers.

Always carefully, delicately, as if he did not wish to offend her, the *ocambo* slid his index finger along the borders of her lips, and then, with medical proficiency, pulled down her lower eyelid.

He turned to face the spectators.

And he nodded his head.

Another man, fat and jolly, egged on by the first, came toward her in short hops, like a tomeguin finch.

Finally he mustered his aplomb and caressed Ada's hair, paternally, affectionately, gazing at her with pity. He let the brilliant red strands slide through his fingers, admiring their texture and color. With almost exaggerated care, he pulled one out. He held it by the ends and stretched it, apparently to test its elasticity.

He then turned and rejoined the eager clan of lustful men.

"To survive," Firefly told himself straightaway, an order dictated by blind prenatal instinct, "I must convince myself that nothing I am seeing or hearing is true. Soon I will realize that I am dreaming, and I will feel the cool varnished wood of the recamier against my feet, the silk rubbing against my sex, and my sex staining it white. That's reality. None of this exists. If I don't believe that, I'm done for."

Wall tiles, with bony dance band

He woke up in a beer hall by the harbor, ignorant of who had brought him there or why. They had set him down in a wicker rocking chair, which was still swaying gently.

Before him was a tall frigid wall mosaic: a brutally realistic portrayal of a big band made up of skeleton musicians perched on kegs of beer or clambering with their pointy elbows and knees up pyramids of chilled bottles overflowing with foam and bearing soggy labels for Hatuey and Polar.

The rumba-dancing skeletons tooted on bamboo flutes, sashayed their sharp hips, strummed raspy guitars with long fingernails black as oxhorn. Several of them chugged entire bottles; others, their empty eye sockets peering at the recipe instructions engraved on a rolling pin, prepared a succulent punch that they adorned with slices of pineapple, gigantic olives, glazed cherries, and even little Chinese parasols that they stuck into a yielding mass of chunky ice cubes.

In front of that garish yet graceful display – scrubbed daily with coal-tar cleanser, or at least so it looked – sporting an indifference or impudence not uncommon among errant and nocturnal people who drift through life with no fixed port, the coachman suddenly appeared. Unbuttoned and unshaven, he looked sleepless, like someone returning from a wake where they served no snacks or from a girl's fifteenth birthday party.

"So, just like in fairy tales . . ." he whispered straight off, coming overly close to Firefly's ear to win an unwarranted confidence, the telltale move of a rascal or a pickpocket. His foul breath flooded the air repeatedly like a haze of bagasse. "What happened afterwards?"

"After what?" Firefly rubbed his eyes.

"After we saw each other, you big oaf." The driver adopted an exaggerated air of mock astonishment. And he began to dig around his teeth with a toothpick.

"This morning . . ."

"Come on, man! You know we saw each other yesterday morning, or doesn't time mean anything to you? Tell me, what happened after that?"

"After . . ." Firefly managed to mumble, but somehow he could not wake up entirely or articulate anything without tripping over his tongue.

A big, smooth-skinned mulatta with green eyes steamed across the beer hall toward the back room or the kitchen. She was dressed as a rumba dancer in a skirt with starched flounces; her belly showed and colored ribbons embellished her billowing sleeves. Around her head was an assembly of metallic curlers held tight by a hairnet with plastic coral-hued flowers.

Struck perhaps by something she had forgotten or needed urgently, she came to an abrupt halt beside a chest, immense and dark like a varnished casket, mahogany with copper hinges. She lifted the lid and, struggling to hold it open, pulled a phonograph from the depths. There was a record already in place, with the attentive and alienated dog of His Master's Voice. Using the fairly rusty lateral crank, she wound it up. Then the scratchy voice of Rita Montaner blossomed.

"Tell me! What's the big mystery?" The coachman stood to take off his black vest, as if he were suddenly suffocating from the heat.

"After that, I went to the tower."

"What tower?"

"The Gothic tower. An elderly girl took me. Down below there's a garden all tiny and wrinkled. There's a red bridge and a waterfall. Old men go there in the morning. They raffle off virgins."

The driver's guffaws echoed all over the beer hall, bouncing off the enamel of the tiles. "Listen to the things this chump thinks up! He's got flowing water in the tower! And if that weren't enough, a virgin nowadays!" He exploded in a scornful cackle.

Firefly flew up from the rocking chair as if someone had dumped it over. He ran for the door, his steps stumbling and awkward, a puppet blind to whoever was pulling the strings. He lunged for the exit like he was desperate for air. Or the truth.

He tripped, recovered, reached the street.

The rumba dancer opened her eyes wide and crossed herself before slapping her open hand on her forehead – the curlers vibrated with a dull tinkling. "Praised be the Holiest!" And she hurried to the bar.

On the beery wall tiles Firefly's shadow had shrunk as he distanced himself from the rocking chair. It looked like a magnet had drawn it to the edge of the mosaic and then deformed and compressed it into a squat fleeing sphere, bluish shot through with blood-orange streaks, vitreous.

The coachman's, on the contrary, loomed larger when he got up with a glass of anisette in his hand, a crosshatched silhouette in the center of the wall superimposed on the case of beer where a skeleton, wearing a crown of orange blossoms and a veil undulating in the breeze, played the harp.

Both shadows abruptly dissolved when the rumba dancer sent the bar's lights into a violent blackout.

Filled with the inextinguishable energy that comes from realizing you have been played for a fool, Firefly continued running down the street. He had no idea why the image he could not shake, even for an instant, was not that of the ignoble auctioneer Munificence offering Ada's innocent body to the highest bidder, rather the opposite, that of Munificence the generous benefactor who had taken him in, the charity-house mentor faking purity, putting on airs, *lying*. "With all the discipline and order she insisted on in the charity house," he said to himself, "there was no way Munificence could be unaware of this open leak, this depravity."

He was fleeing not the driver's convulsive chortles or his licorice stench but that lethal, insufferable image gnawing at him from the inside, emptying his eyes.

He crossed a square, where the cobblestones were drenched as if there had been a sudden shower, then an avenue lined with royal palms, their wilted crowns bowed by a northerly gust. He passed under the elevated trestle made of black wood where the trains from the provinces came in, and he sensed the sharp odor of cane syrup and that red-streak fungus that sours the stalks.

Going over a drawbridge, he heard his own footsteps echoing on the creaky planks as if they belonged to somebody else.

He reached the docks.

What came to mind was an etching that adorned the office of one of the notaries, amid the clammy file folders: a bird's-eye view of the port of Havana. Two contorted angels in the upper corners held a ribbon with a name and a date waving in the island's strong steady breeze . . .

It's going to snow

The wind leaned on the masts, tried to carry off the twisted sails. In the anthill of the docks reigned a restlessness, the sleepwalking chaos that precedes any major disembarkation.

Hordes of rodents, relying on some infallible and gregarious intuition more accurate than all telegraphs put together, had invaded the port's every pipe and sewer the night before, where they awaited the scent of dry grain to launch their assault.

Dropping anchor was a Spanish brigantine from the African coast with a cargo of pure unmixed blacks, who would deliver, according to the prayer in that morning's *Diario de la Marina*, "with the strength of their arms, linked to the fabulous grinding machines of the mills, a decisive boost to the nascent sugar industry."

As the ship rubbed up against the pier, the air was inundated with the rank odor of rot pouring from the hold: a stench of putrid sweat, foul drinking water, rancid urine, spoiled milk, open wounds, and brine.

In between the captain's commands shouted in a thick and despotic Castilian could be heard the creak of the hawsers, the exhilarated cries and euphoric swearing of the sailors on board, and, farther off, the moans of the slaves, the wails, the nasal voices now in exile scolding the gods of the earth for having forsaken them, for leaving them and their families and their animals defenseless against the profiteering gangs of pale-faced traffickers.

Everything was agitation amidships, hither-thither, hurry-hurry. The crewmen, half naked, desiccated, and feverish, ran to the bridge and contemplated the city jubilantly; they pointed at the yellowed and twisted features of the palatial buildings as if these were mirages from their deliria during the passage, or as if they recognized them and were confirming the accuracy of the engravings they had been shown in the mother country to beguile them with the pageantry of America. Then they turned the other way, toward the pink towers of the churches and the light green crowns of the royal palms that swayed like cool sprouting grass the length of the port's boulevard. They ran singing and whistling back to their cabins and tossed bucketfuls of water at one another, swabbing their pale sopping hides now that they no longer had to go even without drinking to make the water last.

Naked but for a cassock with gold braid and buttons that poorly dissembled his well-endowed nether parts, a blond sailor – his long hair agleam like a sulfur flare in the island sun – ran back and forth to the gangway where he piled up his gear: a sack of nougats from Alicante and Jijona whose lumpy riches, the whites and browns of almonds and green walnuts and ground-bee honey, stuck out through the mendings in the fabric; a jug of red wine that projected a trembling amethyst gleam onto the wood of the deck when its owner placed and steadied it as if it were the fragile beaker of an alchemist; a rustic musical instrument, like a violin made of unsanded wood, with an outsized homemade bow; and, finally, a fuming minuscule simian that immediately clambered to the top of the pile and glared every which way while emitting the vainglorious growl of a vigilant proprietor, threatening and rapacious.

Like wildfire in a dry cane field, news of the arrival spread the length of the archways of the port district, where, stacked in a sticky dream of pan sugar and rum, evicted from every tenement, there lived whores during Lent, scarred lepers, vendors of lottery tickets awaiting the jackpot, Soviet advisers, Indians selling sticks of sugarcane and mammees and jerked beef in clay crockery, and a few blacks recently freed, singing country songs and sniffing snuff.

Industrious if still hardly white-skinned landowners in search of grinding hands for their future plantations began crowding the docks, along with belligerent sugar-mill managers and eager traffickers. In the uproar, slavers of all tints mixed in with the lay-abouts and natterers who always hung around the port hoping for a chance to get in on the leftovers of some big scam or the trickle-down from some contraband trade protected by the governor.

In the midst of this tumult, which ought to have provided some distraction but which in reality perturbed him even more, Fire-fly's thoughts returned – the way the threat of dizziness returns or the weedy reek of vomit long after it has disappeared from view – to the image of Ada naked, to the meanness and baseness of the one he had trusted, Munificence, to her unforeseeable wretched-ness and duplicity.

Pervaded by that dizzying stench, he understood how he had been manipulated, how he had been used for years and years, nothing but easy prey for the ringleaders, for their poisonous games, their meticulous effort at pretense.

He did not know which he desired more, to be one of the slaves covered in boils and chains about to climb out of the hold and at least make it clear to himself that he was not the owner of his body or his destiny, or on the contrary to walk along the docks until he reached the reefs, where the roaring waves break in furrows, and there give himself over entirely to the sea, to no longer being.

The return of that revolting vision of Ada, which by then he felt obliged to attribute to reality and not, as ought to have been the case, to the clutter of sullied images that cloud a hangover, made the human species seem like irredeemable debris, rubbish. That was it: the dregs, the remains of an ideal creature fashioned in the beginning by some deluded god, and in the end reduced to this prattling pantomime, to this essential filth.

Meanwhile, a few proper ladies began turning up, their faces masked by finely wrought mother-of-pearl fans, who without leaving their carriages sought to acquire newly arrived black girls for domestic service before they could be spoiled by libertarian excesses, or by the lust for suicide and flight that had already ruined the help in more than one palatial home and poisoned the crew in more than one peaceable work camp, thereby populating the already vermin-infested jungle with bloodthirsty Maroons bent on vengeance, primed for murderous raids on the plantations.

The shenanigans that followed put the finishing touch on the mayhem. Amid a storm of blue crates falling every which way, dumped by drunken cabin boys who could not have cared less (a pulley gave way and a big-screen television shattered against a mast), ahead of the slaves themselves, appeared the frenzied salesmen of the coveted merchandise that everyone dreamed of bidding on and profiting by.

Down the gangway came an auctioneer.

His large bare feet were covered with sores and black goop. His tight pants were leather. On his chest the green waving lines of his tattoos, intertwined serpents and ciphers, glistened in the sun like emerald threads. He raised his right hand to ask for silence from the landowners jostling for a spot in a semi-circle around the boarding ramp. Then with the irksome grandiloquence of an Arab storyteller arriving at an oasis, to the four winds he proffered a rotund "Do I hear more?" before reciting seemingly by heart a long inventory of embellished claims for the human product he had brought to market, still healthy despite the seas, robust even, ever potent.

"Big bruiser, nice and dark, dirty, bearded, long-faced Mozambican with tribal tattoos on his face, really wide feet, he's got all his teeth, sways as he walks . . .

"Civilized black from the Angolan nation, named Juan, dark as they come, with a bit of a beard, huge, with big eyes . . .

"Antonio, black from the Coast with three scars on his face and missing the nail on his left big toe, falsetto voice, a dirty-black color . . .

"Black woman from Angola with plenty of milk, no vices, pretty-faced, slurs her R's when she speaks . . ."

Firefly could not go on listening to the auctioneer, much less to his own morbidly repetitious thoughts. Coming toward him, seeming to surge out of the cluster of slavers, snowy, unpolluted amid the dross, seeking him out with that glassy, pinkish stare he would have recognized anywhere, was the pasty skin-and-bones girl, sent yet again, he told himself, by the harshest orishas, the ones that unmask certain men so they can assail their dim-witted credulity with the intolerable truth.

Her shining dress and her scaly anemic whiteness, the agility with which she slid among the traffickers like a cold-blooded reptile guided solely by the vibrations of her prey, the aureole that surrounded her – all these were accentuated by the sun to the point of hallucination: the unreal that emerges when it is clearest, when it is brightest.

Behind her, the blacks were climbing out of the hold, chained, thirsty; they moaned and squeezed shut their eyes, blinded by the razor's edge of tropical light. Mice with phosphorescent eyes skimmed along fast as arrows.

Unseeing, unerring instinct having carried her to his side, Firefly could scrutinize her more closely than ever: the livid face and each matted albino lock magnified by excessive proximity or by the sharpness of perception that all repugnance sparks.

He discovered something that until now had escaped him, he could not say why: The scrawny girl had no eyelashes. The discovery left him trembling, as if a deep-sea fish, wriggling, gelatinous, had slithered past him.

Without any reference to what had occurred or even so much as a hello, the elderly child beamed an ironic rictus in his direction, which for her perhaps corresponded to a smile.

"Want to see her again?" her nasal singsong challenged. "Want to know where she ended up? Look for her in the purple house, the one where two canals meet. She's there, waiting for you."

The sky once again grew ugly. Tenebrous nimbus clouds, silvery-gray and edged with gold, began piling high in spinning updrafts approaching from the east. Gusts, crafty and freezing, blew in from the north. From the west, a whirling downdraft. To cap it off, from the south came that strange sound the whole city had heard once before a long time ago.

"It's the souls coming back," one of the proper ladies averred, forsaking for a moment her mother-of-pearl fan to cross herself.

"It's not that, your ladyship," replied the coachman respectfully, though certain of what he was saying and even with a trace of authority. "It's going to snow."

The Pavilion of the Pure Orchid

He believed in the furtive midget's latest revelation, even if it was offered only for the appalling gratification of mocking him, or for the more benign pleasure of engaging in sheer malice with no risk of reprimand, human or divine.

He fled the port by sea, crossing the thick churning waters of the bay in a rickety launch packed with pilgrims fulfilling promises and with drunks who chugged precipitous cups of oysters on the pier and lukewarm cans of beer during the crossing, which they then tossed overboard to see how they bounced off the propeller's foamy wake.

He disembarked on the other side of the bay, seized by an excruciating bout of seasickness. Tottering under the archways, he made his way through the barrio of the Santeria priests. Pale young mulattos in underpants and T-shirts, yawning and mussed, used one hand to calm the bulge in their crotches, insubordinate at that hour, and the other to smooth their reddish frizz, stiff and coiled like the strikers on flint lighters, before plunging into sweeping the entire block with thatch brooms, then giving it a soak with buckets of water to settle the "duss."

The board windows of the vast azure homes were already swinging open to reveal lights inside: fresh candles twinkled on altars surrounded by sky-blue silks, turquoise beads, and little piles of finely ground indigo. He watched someone emerge from a brick courtyard and roam through rooms of assorted colors and clarities.

Firefly made his way deeper into the part of the city where land mixes with water.

Long covered boardwalks painted an intense violet-blue, like they had been rubbed with indigo, were slowly sinking into the swamp. The rambling houses on stilts, which looked to be perforated on all sides so as not to be so stifling, gave the impression they were floating, swaying slightly, hushed, always nocturnal, always alone. They were excessively large for the few who resigned themselves to a life plagued by mosquitoes on those sweltering and pestilent mudflats.

Only the gulls, always quick to ingest the refuse with which the fishing families polluted the waters, vied for the houses. They nested on the roofs and soon covered them with their excretions, forming veritable hummocks, irregular and grayish-brown, like bloated towers that at dusk turned the abodes into fossil out-crops or whimsical dunes or mosques dreamed up by demented architects.

Narrow semicircular canals, imperfectly laid out, formed a sloppy labyrinth through the neighborhood. The big houses were scattered according to the capricious law of mudslides or what-ever potential opportunistic builders might have seen in preexist-ing rubble. Anemic laky waves, seemingly roused by some distant shudder, now and again agitated the dense waters and caused them to glisten like tarnished aluminum, ashen gray.

Firefly, frantically seeking the place where two canals meet, hurried down the rickety boardwalks that zigzagged from one sprawling house to the next, but the semicircles never converged. Having forgotten fatigue and hunger, he now ignored the cool downpour that began to pelt the mudflats. He thought about the yard with the chamber pot, shaded by the red flowers of the royal poinciana, so cozy and warm, and then, as if everything were bub-bling up in his memory, he recalled the hospice courtyard and the spray of water from its fountain. The stocks did not come to mind.

He continued trudging along the boardwalks suspended over the muck, cobbled together with flimsy planks and wobbly, poorly anchored pillars, very high above the water. These wooden paths were not straight, rather they converged and forked with no apparent motive, perhaps following the precarious solidity of the ground or the convenience of the impromptu mullet fishermen, hungry for the oily opalescent eggs, who with nothing more than a lantern and a hammock occupied the derelict houses during the season and vacated them as soon as the ban was declared.

Suddenly, several of the creaking walkways seemed to flow into one, wider and more solid than the others, made with sturdier crossbeams. In the distance, sinking into the sea, or into that mortar of brine and silt that took its place on the nearby horizon, he could make out an enormous house, fixed up not long ago and slathered with garish colors.

These were not canals the way the lunar herald had announced; more like mud creeks, thinner and more fluid than the rest of the bog.

Firefly picked up his pace. He was zipping along now, closing in on the lurid purple doorway, anxious to read the words engraved on a vertical piece of varnished wood carved in undulations, like a prayer flag, when an ill-fated skid sent him face-first into the muck.

He started flapping his arms, as if anyone could swim in that slime. He was sinking. He knew that he had to hold still, that every attempt to rise up would bury him further. Carefully he stretched one leg, then the other. But he could not bring himself any closer to the posts holding up the boardwalk, though they were nearly within reach, an arm's length away.

His body was a thing apart, a rough and shoddy entity he neither felt nor wished to feel.

The muscles in his arms were useless. For an instant, he imagined them bulging and covered in tattoos; he dreamed his body was obeying him, climbing effortlessly up to the boardwalk. He breathed deeply. He stiffened up. He remembered the stepladder he had mounted as a child in order to describe the hurricane.

Then he realized how alone he was. Unless he managed to clamber up on that boardwalk, no one would rescue him and he would sink for good into the mud, into the rot.

He tried to call for help, knowing it was useless.

Such a familiar failure: He opened his mouth and nothing came out.

He decided to wait. To attempt no movement. His body became somehow undifferentiated, mixed in with the slime and of the same texture. All he had to do was stop breathing and thinking to become forever one with the bog; he was already an inert substance, scum in the scum.

For Firefly an entire day went by, even if in the crude ticking of clocks the interval lasted only an hour. He thought he would never reach those posts, that he would become completely immobilized, a stone statue fallen into the muck centuries ago. He was crying, he realized. He had no idea how much time had truly passed.

The surface of the mud was swarming. Thousands of iridescent green insects with gigantic legs and filigreed wings jumped and chased each other on the thin mossy coating; others navigated slowly, sliding in pairs along minuscule shoots from one lily pad to the next.

A frog jumped.

The sun began to go down.

Firefly opened his eyes, perhaps to hear better.

He turned his head. Yes, it was the distant roar of a motor. A small boat was approaching from the sea.

"A drowned man!" yelled one of the crew. "A drowned man!"

Firefly recognized them right off. In taking away his sense of direction, Mother Nature – always stingy in her consolations – had given him the ability to recognize anyone immediately, no matter if he had only laid eyes on him once and just for a moment. In this instance, he was certain that both of them had been in the basement of the Gothic tower.

They pointed at him from afar with curiosity bordering on disgust; he might have been a beached shark. Between sneering jibes, they fished him out, sopping and silent.

"Just what you deserve, kid, so you'll learn not to get drunk and wander about alone in places like this!" one shouted at him.

"Come off it, pal," replied the other. "You can see he's old enough for that! He wasn't going to spend his whole life jerking himself off!"

The man was wearing nothing but a bathing suit and a thick silver chain bearing a charm. He was emaciated. His cranium shone with the morbid gleam of tanning oil. His flesh was milky and insipid.

The other, redheaded and freckled, came armored with a baseball cap and green sunglasses, a big flowery shirt, very tight white pants, and canvas shoes.

Once they had deposited Firefly in one of the white seats of their impeccable launch, like a freshly caught porgy left to suffocate on dry land, they carried on with the taunts, since watching him gasp for breath seemed to amuse them.

"Have some rum to warm up. Though you must be pretty warm already to end up down there, right?" They cracked up.

"I . . . I was looking for the big house," Firefly tried to explain. "A big house where two canals meet."

"Aha! So you don't know your way around here and don't even have a clue what's what! Then what were you doing here alone at this time of day, girlie? Fishing around for the big bullfrog?" More cackles.

"Enough, cut the clowning," the bald one decided. "If you want to go into the pavilion, we'll take you. That's why we're members and come whenever we feel like it. Though we always take the boat, not like you dragging yourself through the mud. Dry yourself off with this sponge. And here, put on a clean T-shirt."

Only then did Firefly grasp what he had seen carved on the placard by the door: THE PAVILION OF THE PURE ORCHID.

They took hold of the wooden banner and yanked on it, like they were milking a cow. Far away, deep inside the ramshackle house, maybe at the back of a kitchen filled with sacks of flour or perhaps only muffled by the sticky, ever-present humidity, a little bell rang, dark and dull like the low keys on a marimba.

When the new owners christened the house, they must have scraped the placard with the tip of a jackknife; underneath the letters of the new name a few of the previous ones were still visible in elegant, sparkling gold loops: THE . . . IDEA.

Two metal lounge chairs, rusted and unusable, their once-perfect springs now greenish-black and bunched up, flanked the heavy repainted door, which was perforated near the top by a deep peephole like a miniature spyglass. Quietly swaying to the rhythm of the breeze like bunches of charred garlic heads, bat colonies hung from the eaves.

Three bolts rattled: the first a rough rasp like a horseshoe clattering against red marble; the next two soft glides like the trigger on an antique revolver.

A black man opened the door.

His cheeks and forehead were covered in tribal tattoos.

He looked the three of them over from head to toe, and considered before offering a perfunctory, nearly inaudible, "Gentlemen, come in." Either he was not sure he recognized them or he recalled from the last visit their less than adequate tips. Thinking it over, he added in a dry cutting tone, "Are you certain that the youngster is old enough to do us the honor of a visit? Do you know the baron? Would you like me to call him right now?"

"The youngster?" the bald one erupted, huffy and scornful. "Take a good look, and if that won't do then give him a feel. Come on, in the crotch and you'll see!" He grabbed hold of the Dahomean's arm and started pulling on it.

The doorman, maybe worried about herpes, snatched it back; Firefly had turned bright red and was covering his nether parts

[159]

to ward off the clutch. The redhead raised his hands to his head, then jerked his right thumb at his mouth to indicate to the somber acolyte the drunken cause of such immoderation.

Inside, a cockpit was the first thing that came to Firefly's mind. It was a big circular wooden structure open to the tiled roof with a chandelier in the center. Along the outer edges, crudely sewn folding screens made of nun-gray sugar sacks formed slapdash cells that hugged the walls haphazardly, shabby little rooms that looked ready to collapse at the slightest jostle.

Gigantic tree ferns: that was what stood out in the middle. A fern jungle, whose wrinkled leaves sheltered the fraying damask and gold threads of a curved sofa. Two white platforms, each with lateral stages like those used for Olympic champions, flanked this ridiculous piece of furniture.

In the middle of each cell – now that the gloom had dissipated and he could see – lay a large wicker lounge chair, sagging or wobbly, and next to it a night table of the same weave bearing a glass, an ashtray, and an oval bottle filled with mint liqueur.

"Gentlemen, please be seated," the tattooed man invited. "The booths are individual. I shall bring you ice in a moment."

Off he went down a hallway, but not before encouraging Firefly, who by all appearances looked terrified. "And you, young man, don't be so afraid of being seen. Here no one gets eaten.

You can have a wonderful time all by yourself; everyone minds his own business and that's all there is to it . . . One thing, and don't ever forget it since you're new: one looks but one does not touch. *Plaisir des yeux*," he added, snooty and churlish, no doubt quoting some madame who had once visited the island.

He returned shortly, distributed the ritual refreshments, and carefully closed the folding screens. In the damp, soiled fabric crisscrossed with stitches only a single slit remained, offering a view of the improvised stage.

The moment the partitions shut, Firefly felt a gratuitous fear of being closed in, just as one day in the shade of the royal poinciana he had felt afraid of being out in the open.

The discomfort was very familiar; he resigned himself to suffering it once more.

A few tambourines sounded.

The ferns moved slightly, suggesting a wayward bird flitting from branch to branch, or an impossible sea breeze breaching the wall.

It was neither: parting the greenery were big strapping young mulattos crowned with laurel wreaths and garbed in light-blue Greek tunics and sandals. The youngest, a good-looking buck, held aloft a lyre.

They occupied the platforms, exhibiting the Ionic manners and sepia poise of an old Sicilian photograph.

On the highest stages on either side of the sofa, somber teenagers pretended to play the sistrum, like Arcadian shepherds lost in the bog, whose noxious vapors kept spoiling the scene. On the lateral platforms, seated without much conviction, practically loafing, the tambourine players officiated.

The refreshments, like some vegetarian's transgression, all contained pork: soaked in honey, wrapped in guava or basil leaves, fried rinds or with cassava, each of them flecked with the fresh greenery of Spanish fly.

Firefly tried to wipe off the snacks, but the pinching bitter taste still came through. So he drank an entire glass of the mint liqueur, warm – the waiter, of course, had forgotten the ice.

The tambourines stopped.

A teenage girl appeared, practically a child, a mulatta with green eyes and cinnamon skin. From chin to ankles she was covered in dense necklaces, thick amber charms, golden seashells, and fresh sunflowers, so many that her body seemed bent under the weight. They had painted her eyebrows with cinnabar, her cheeks with eggshell. Her mouth was white. She smiled. She was a mahogany

sculpture, loaded down with offerings, rising amid the big ado-
lescents in profile.

As soon as they saw her, the brown boys began fondling themselves, as if the mulatta's body, beyond being a display of purity
and nakedness, was the cue for an encounter among boys, the
go-ahead for a slight shock. More: for an orgy.

In the middle of the stage, a tall fleshless man with sharp bones
and a sallow complexion, shuffling awkwardly in sandals, handed
the lads little tubs or rather pouches sheathed in snakeskin and
overflowing with fresh green crushed herbs, moist and poisonous.

He distributed the soft containers, then with his index finger
he caressed his own upper lip out to his cheekbone, apparently
trying to remove an invisible stain, or to smooth the rough edges
of an ugly scar.

It was Gator.

And the fat man at his side, wrapped in a sticky toga, his feet
bare and swollen, could be none other than Isidro.

During a break from the tambourines, Firefly heard, or
believed he heard, a conversation between the two weasels.

"What's up?" Isidro yelled, gesturing wildly, flushed by the
herbs or by the porky refreshments with Bacardi. "Hasn't the
new one shown her face?"

[163]

"I don't know what the fuck is wrong with her," Gator answered hotly. "She should be here any minute."

"So what are you going to call her?" asked Isidro mischievously.

"Hada. Her real name."

"We've got to change that."

In that in-between zone, when surfacing from sleep but not yet fully awake, images can get condensed into words that seem entirely made up of sounds or silences. Just like that, Firefly, his face pressed against the slit in the grimy folding screen, saw: THEY TRICKED YOU.

The piercing whistle of the letters shattered his eardrums, wove a red-hot net inside his body that set him aflame.

Then something even more powerful than those tiny blazing threads shook him from stem to stern. Another image, as unreal and as substantive as the previous, appeared on the very same stage: *Ada naked*, offered up for ogling, the pretext for the old weasels' solitary fondling.

He felt a bitter wave rise into his mouth, green like the herbs, weedy and rank. He tried to think about another green: the ceiba tree next to the fishpond, filtering white vertical light. A lethal lava burned in his stomach. Then he saw the girl seem to look up at the heavens, or at the glass chandelier that occupied their celestial place on the cockpit's ceiling. Her eyes were opaque and dry, her gestures dull, her steps awkward and slow.

The big boys, without interrupting the tambourine beat, dipped the tips of their fingers into something gooey at the bottom of the little sacks and licked them as if they were secretly sucking on nectar's essence.

Gator approached the young woman. Carefully, almost respectfully, performing the prescribed ritual of a sacred ceremony as it were, he spread that thick golden jelly extracted from the hearts of herbs on the tips of her breasts, on the barely shadowed triangle of her sex.

Firefly closed his eyes. He surprised himself by praying for the very first time in his life: "Dear God, please make all this a hallucination, a drunken mirage, let me awaken right now somewhere else, let the name I heard not be Ada's, let it not be her, let it not be that they auctioned her off in the tower for this, *let none of this be real.*"

Then, as if possessed by a reckless demon, Gator grabbed the dark pouch from the youngest of the tambourine players and buried his entire hand in it. He spread the stuff all over his own sharp features, trembling, licking his palm, caressing anxiously, almost voluptuously, the invisible scar on his cheekbone.

Soon he raised his hand in the air, where it shook Parkinson's-like while he sketched something out or signaled a terse order. His glistening fingers quivered with infinitesimal movements, each independent of the others: five henchmen utterly liberated.

Now Firefly thought he saw – or maybe it was the mint liqueur – Ada's body superimposed on the mulatta's, confused with hers as if they were but one.

She looked like a sleepwalker.

She moved among the performers with a sluggishness that was supposed to be lascivious and was just dreary, to the point of being nightmarish.

She wiggled her hips in a drowsy dance, her blank gaze following a dot that floated in the air and fell in long swoops like a dying bird.

Firefly began to cry.

Gator's consorts did not touch the sleepwalker while she slid among them, nor did they even look at her. They continued beating their tambourines and with the tips of their fingers they groped their own nipples, as if they were checking how hard they were. They laughed again and again.

What – the question set Firefly's body atremble – were the occupants of the booths doing when she approached the folding screens and they could almost touch her, could breathe in her aroma through the slits?

Then the dancer, perhaps following a discernible route known by all, approached his screen and Firefly could only look into her eyes and feel his own well up.

"Ada," he said between sobs, believing at that moment it was her, "how could it be?"

The girl, who undoubtedly could barely hear over the tambourines drowning out his voice, and who in the most obvious way possible was looking anywhere but at the slits, paying the booths not the slightest attention, seemed nevertheless to understand him. Her eyes paused for a moment, rapt, fixed on something in the emptiness and (this is what Firefly believed) she also began to cry.

A thought struck him in the midst of that tumult, the coup de grace: Suppose his own sister were one of the "models" in these repugnant tableaus?

Suddenly he lashed out with his fist against the screen, against the insufferable image of that body, sullied and naked, dumped into a feeble life of sleepwalking for the *ocambos*.

The hulking contraption collapsed. Beyond the flattened wreck of scrap wood and rags, abruptly in place of the vanished mulatta who must have been hauled off, stood Gator shuddering with rage. A smear of cinnabar on his forehead made him look even more misshapen than usual.

"Man is the shit of the universe," Firefly told himself. And he stopped punching.

It was useless. On his other side, like a spring released, stood the Dahomean servant, this time carrying not a snack but an enormous maul, like a ritual weapon wrapped in bandage tape. The white strips, Firefly realized immediately, were stained light brown from dried excrement or coagulated blood.

Gator's face, observing the coming reprimand from a few steps away, turned deep violet, became elongated, convulsive (or at least that is what Firefly saw, in what may not have been a nightmare, although it obeyed the same rules); his harelip mouth opened and closed in an inaudible wail.

The tambourine players picked up the pace of their banging and thumping, filling Firefly's ears with a frenetic, deafening drumming intended to drive the listener crazy.

"You see this?" was all the befuddled famulus said to the harried fly. "You want it up your ass?" He brandished the maul, then paused for a threatening moment. "Or would you rather I split your skull in two and dump you overboard so you'll rot in the swamp, you faggot bastard?"

Firefly did not answer. He looked quickly and for the last time toward the center of the room. Just like the mulatta's beforehand, the bodies of Isidro and Gator had evaporated. He had the sudden impression that everything was calming down. Fed up with one another, or with the pointed one-act farce they probably put on every day, the boys were lying on the floor, sandals off, using their tambourines for pillows; they had stopped their caressing and each lay alone, his Greek tunic wrapped around him like a comfy nightshirt.

Firefly recalled the time as a child in the leper clinic when he jumped like a windup toy to launch his awkward flight and got spattered with the lumpy noxious liquid from an enema. He felt trapped and alone. He saw himself sliding down the cistern on the chamber pot. He felt watched as he shat, the butt of the furious ruffian's ridicule.

And he took off, running crazily toward the middle of the cockpit, toward the ferns.

He bounded over two of the exhausted ephebes, who turned over with vigorous snores, like disturbed animals, and ended up sleeping in each other's arms.

Beyond two plaster columns he crossed a stuffy storage loft held up by cardboard boxes and crammed full of tunics. Through a door open a crack, he spied the sea.

He ran along the wooden pier. He looked back. No one was following.

He thought he heard the tambourines start up. Or maybe it

was the motor of a far-off boat, nocturnal defectors trying, despite the radar's watchful eye, to escape the island.

He breathed deeply, looked up at the heavens filled with stars gathered in calm spirals.

Only then did he notice he was injured. He could not say when it happened or what had caused it: his arms and feet were bleeding.

"These wounds," he said out loud, "will not heal. They are *the marks of mendacity*, the signatures on my body of disgrace."

A putrid stench rose up from the swamp. Iridescent white animals, creeping and viscous, somewhere between lizard, eel, and snake, wriggled over the weeds and bare patches of the bog.

A bolt of lightning traced a golden ideogram on the horizon.

The reptiles wrapped themselves around each other with short snapping sounds, knotted themselves to each other in repugnant couplings or petty scuffles, entanglings they then tried to undo with slippery somersaults and spastic contractions.

Everyone deceived. Everything nauseated. But deep down, he told himself, he was thankful: he had seen the true face of man, his essential duplicity, his *need*, as unquenchable as hunger or thirst, for trickery, for wretchedness.

Now he knew people were capable of anything: of selling off father and mother, of turning over to the Inquisition and the stake the one they were pretending to protect. Capable of treachery, of usury with their loved ones. Of lies.

He lay facedown on the creaking dock.

He put his head over the edge.

To throw up.

He swore he would return to exterminate them all. And himself along with them, and thus cleanse the universe of so much dung. He certainly knew where to get rat poison and how to mix it with rum so no one could tell.

He turned over on his back.

In the sky, the fiery constellations seemed to spin.

archipelago books

is a not-for-profit literary press devoted to
promoting cross-cultural exchange through innovative
classic and contemporary international literature
www.archipelagobooks.org